The Diary of Lillie Langtry
And Other Remembrances

The Diary of
Lillie Langtry
And Other Remembrances

A Novel By
Donna Lee Harper

ARROWHEAD CLASSICS, INC.
LOS ANGELES

This edition published by Arrowhead Classics, Inc.

1995 Arrowhead Classics Books

ISBN 1-886571-00-7
Library of Congress Catalog Card Number: 94-073387

Printed and bound in the United States of America

7 6 5 4 3

To My Mother

Table of Contents

Foreword

I like Lillie Langtry. I never met the lady — she preceded me by almost one hundred years — but after reading about her, I feel like I know her. And I like her. Not only because she was beautiful and talented, which she certainly was, but most of all because she was bright. Extremely so. And ahead of her times by almost a century.

Lillie (not *Lily,* which she did not like), was a child of the Victorian era, no question about that. But she was also a major player in the battle for women's rights, a struggle that was in its earliest stages in her days.

Born Emily Charlotte Le Breton at St. Helier on the Channel Island of Jersey on October 13, 1853, Lillie was a beauty from infancy. So much so that while she was just into her teens an army officer proposed marriage to her, only to be rebuffed because she was so young. Lillie was awe struck by London when taken there by her mother on her first trip to that city and vowed to return only after she was familiar with the social graces she was so lacking at the time.

She not only returned to London a few years later — as the young bride of Edward Langtry — but took the city by storm. Her overwhelming beauty soon had every artist and photographer in the city clamoring to have her pose for them. She became the darling of London high society and was on the guest list for every important party in town. She soon caught the eye of Albert Edward, the Prince of Wales, and began a relationship with the future king of England that was to endure for years.

Edward Langtry, never one for the society whirl, soon withdrew more and more into the background, and Lillie's marriage quickly faded into estrangement. But Edward stubbornly refused to give Lillie a divorce and was not even aware that she gave birth to a daughter that some gossips said was sired by the Prince himself.

Lillie realized that life as the favorite grande dame of high society would be short-lived and vowed to go to work and earn herself a living.

One friend suggested she become an artist, another thought she should become a landscape architect. But it took her best friend, Oscar Wilde, to guide Lillie into a career which was to make her famous — the theater.

She never became an accomplished actress and she knew it. But the crowds came, oh, how they came. It seems everyone wanted to get an in-person glimpse of the now famous "Jersey Lily." She packed them in no matter where she played and even though the critics were oftentimes less than complimentary, her audiences nevertheless loved her. And it didn't hurt to have the once and future king, Edward (and oftentimes his wife Alexandra), in their private box, cheering Lillie on.

Lillie didn't rest on her laurels. She went to Paris and studied under the best acting teacher she could find. But better yet, she was smart enough to form her own company, thus insuring that the majority of the immense profits she was bringing in would go into her bank account and not into that of some unscrupulous promoter.

Her fame had preceded her to America when she went on her first cross-country tour of the U.S. in 1882. She stayed for five years, and knocked them dead from New York to San Francisco and every city and hamlet in between.

By now she was traveling in her own specially built railroad car, the seventy-five foot "Lalee," which had every comfort, including a private bedroom for Lillie, a kitchen, maid's quarters, rooms for her staff and a cozy living room complete with piano.

Lillie not only conquered American audiences, she bought up part of the country as she traveled. A ranch in California — it still exists today as the Langtry Ranch but under a different owner — land in Chicago and a home in New York were just part of her numerous acquisitions.

She was friends with people who today we just read about in the history books — Presidents U. S. Grant and Teddy Roosevelt; Winston Churchill; Rudyard Kipling; George Bernard Shaw; Sarah Bernhardt; Mark Twain; Diamond Jim Brady; P. T. Barnum; the list is endless. Somerset Maugham, who met her on board ship when she was in her sixties, said that when he first approached her from behind he thought she was a woman no older than thirty.

Lillie would have been right at home with today's health fanatics. She jogged two miles every morning, ate only healthy food and had an exquisite figure on her tall five-foot-eight frame.

Lillie was wealthy enough in the 1890s to buy her own theater in London. She was also sending monthly checks to her estranged husband, Edward, who had become an alcoholic. After he died, Lillie married Sir Hugo Gerald de Bathe in 1899 and thereafter possessed the one thing in life that had so far eluded her — a title.

She continued to use the name Mrs. Langtry professionally, but she was now Lady de Bathe in private life. She made five lengthy tours of the U.S. over a period of thirty-five years, and even made a motion picture in New York on her last trip. She owned one of the largest racing stables in England, bred horses in the U.S. and won several important stakes races in Europe. And she was not above winning some big wagers at the same time.

Lillie retired from the stage while in her sixties and moved to Monaco where she spent her remaining years tending her garden and going to parties in Monte Carlo. She died at the age of seventy-six on February 12, 1929, and was buried at the place of her birth on the Isle of Jersey.

She lived a storybook life. She was quite a lady.

— Frank J. Stevens
Sedona, Arizona, 1995

THE DIARY OF LILLIE LANGTRY

1

Welcome to Paradise

*California! What a magnificent combination of climate and
beauty. I took heed of Horace Greeley's advice to "Go West"
and indeed not only went in that direction but purchased a
part of it as well.*

I am thankful that things went so well during my early
tours of the United States. My income was abundant,
allowing me to exercise some business endeavors that
with less funding might have not been possible.

It was during my second season that I had my first
glimpse of the West Coast and California in particular. The
land was perhaps the most beautiful I have ever seen and
the glorious climate made the place a paradise on earth. It
did not take me long to decide to purchase some property
in this wonderful part of the world. It would be a place,
perhaps, that I could escape to and simply rest and enjoy
the scenery. And, admittedly, it would not displease me if
I were to turn a tidy profit on the sale of the property at
some propitious moment in the future.

I was fortunate to have such an eminent personage as
General Barnes, who was a lawyer of high repute, searching
out the ideal piece of land for me to purchase.

Perhaps my heart took charge of my head, because the land I eventually decided upon was truly a gamble as an investment, but, as I was making money "hand over fist," as they say, it seemed not unwise to take the chance. Besides, General Barnes advised me that there was a distinct possibility that a railroad would be passing through the ranch property, thereby notably increasing its value and potential. (I should insert here what, in reality, I found — a few hundred yards of abandoned grading and a prediction that work on the rail line would never be resumed. Writing this long after the fact, I must sorrily admit the prediction came true.)

But, be that as it may, I undauntedly went ahead with the purchase of 6500 acres of land in an area well Southeast of San Francisco and relatively close to Sacramento. The acreage comprised of two arable farms with good ranch houses and a vineyard and cottage, all well-stocked and in working order. Upon my acquiring the property, it became known as "Langtry Farms," which name it retains to this day.

My eight month U.S. tour ended in San Francisco, where I spent two weeks. All of my spare time was devoted to the purchase of furniture for one of my newly acquired ranch houses. Keep in mind this was all done sight unseen, but though I had not actually visited the place, my taste in furniture would not be altered after seeing it, so it was not as difficult a task as it might have seemed.

I disbanded my company of actors and decided, at long last, to not only visit the ranch but to take a much-needed vacation there. The ever efficient Beverly took charge of getting the furniture shipped to the ranch and in company with a group of friends, with much anticipation, we proceeded in the direction of the property.

We were all eager for an early start, and by sunrise we were riding my private railroad car, the Lalee, on our way to what I originally thought was a gigantic lake. Later, I was informed it was actually the Pacific Ocean which had formed what is called San Francisco Bay. Our whole train with the exception of the engine was ferried across the bay in about an hour to the city of Oakland. From there we proceeded to the end of the line, a small village called St. Helena. The nearest major town was Sacramento, which lay in a beautiful valley some 80 miles to the Southeast.

To my surprise, we found a situation which I must secretly admit pleased me: the St. Helena depot was crowded inside and out with people who had come only to see me. Autograph seekers, presents of flowers, fruit and candy and offers of hospitality were the order of the day. The wonderful Californians were now dearer to my heart than ever!

Out of the crowd came Beverly, looking like a fish out of water in his proper English-butler apparel. He had come to meet us with two private stagecoaches which, he informed me, I owned — he had commandeered them from my newly acquired ranch and each coach was pulled by a team of six reliable horses and driven by very determined-looking drivers.

But my devoted fans — I could not bring it upon myself to leave them so soon after arriving and so I signed more autographs than I could count and invited them to an impromptu tea aboard the Lalee. Finally, it was time to go, and here I was, the "Jersey Lily," many thousands of miles from home on the Isle of Jersey in the English Channel, about to take my first stagecoach ride in the Wild West!

I had not realized how long the trip would be. Seventeen miles over a corkscrew road, up a mountain and thence into

3

the valley below — this was the journey that lay ahead before I would finally see my long-anticipated new property.

The exact location of the ranch is in Lake County and it is formed by a fertile plateau of arable and grass land in the Howell Mountains. The road, if I dare call it such, was rough and narrow, and the springs of the coaches being made of leather tongs provided less than a smooth ride. But this was the West, my friends, and we were soon to be an integral part of it. The beauty of the rivers and gorges, flanked by an abundance of green trees, made every bump and thump well worth it. And, as we descended the mountain and got our first panoramic view of my property, it could only be described as a dream of loveliness.

It was early July and vast masses of ripe golden corn waved in the light summer breeze. Here and there, enormous ageless evergreen oak trees stood like welcoming sentinels to our eager party. It was, without exaggeration, an entrancing sight to behold.

In the distance, on the far side of the land, I could see mountains that reminded me of the Swiss Alps — hazy and blue. Numerous cattle ranged near them and, Beverly later informed me, the distant mountains were the boundary of my land and the cattle were mine.

As we continued to drive closer and closer to the heart of the property I became all the more enchanted. There were vineyards, then peach orchards laden with fruit. I had, indeed, made a good choice of land to purchase.

We finally came upon the house. It was exactly what one would want in such a setting. Built entirely of wood, it was not pretentious by any stretch of the imagination, but it was fairly roomy and stood rather high on piles. There was no garden, but, instead, one side had a fenced area which I later learned was used to corral and punch horses and cattle after a round up. A crowd of nonchalant lounging cowboys, picturesquely clothed in red or khaki flannel shirts and leather bead-embroidered trousers, some on ponies, others on foot, loitered near the front door. They looked askance at me, still in my quite proper city attire, but welcomed Beverly as if he were an old friend. As we were all quite exhausted from our stagecoach ride, we quickly went inside.

The ground floor was comprised of a large living room, into which the house-door directly opened. A dining room and kitchen were to the rear. A staircase from the former led to a galley running entirely around it, on to which doors of the bedrooms opened, no space being wasted in halls and passages.

Beverly had seen to it that dinner was served without keeping us waiting and I must say the early start and events of the day had built up a healthy appetite in all of us. We were served trout, beef and quail, all from the ranch and prepared by Indian squaws from the nearby reservation. There were no white servants, male or female, to be found in this remote location. I found it interesting that during the time I was on the ranch the squaws came in relays, working only long enough to earn two or three days' pay. Then, they would spend the money on whatever needs they may have had — women are typical the world over, are they not?

My love of horses was not the only encouragement I needed to get up at daybreak, quickly eat breakfast, and then, dressed cowboy style in shirt, breeches and long moccasins as protection from rattlesnakes, gallop about on a cowpony, exploring every corner of the land.

It was my desire to turn the ranch into a first class stud farm where we could raise race horses of the highest quality. To that end, I engaged an overseer who had managed Haggin's well known stud farm in the East. We found some fine pasture land and he advised me to purchase and import an English stallion named Friar Tuck, by Hermit. He was also anxious to buy some brood mares and it was his plan to sell the offspring for a large profit. The good fellow meant well, but the progeny were not successful in their racing endeavors in California nor elsewhere, and my experiences as a horse breeder proved to be quite costly.

But I had more than enough to take my mind off the lack of success with my race horses. I planned to build several roads on the property which would be lined with eucalyptus trees. Gardens galore for all purposes would be added and the house would be redesigned to make it a really comfortable one.

"Liberty" seems to be a favorite word of Western folk and my cowboys, of every nationality imaginable, including Chinese, walked in and out of my house in search of whatever they needed. Indians from the reservation rode over the property at will from dawn to sunset, with rifles slung on their backs, shooting the game and fishing the trout. Some of the neighboring ranchers, out of the kindness of their hearts, shot my deer out of season and presented them to me in token of welcome. Squatters annexed cows clearly marked with the brand of the ranch. This was basic communism at its best!

Wildlife, of course, abounded on the ranch and several times I found a fawn, which I later learned was tame, wandering around the house. It was not bashful about lying on my bed with its forelegs crossed around my ever-so-patient cat's neck.

There were black bears in the mountains, hares, rabbits and partridge-like crested quail. We all took part in the interesting process of corralling the different herds of cattle and the round up of the horses. Viewing the livestock at close quarters was particularly interesting and we counted eighty horses of all sizes, ages, and shapes, plus many mules.

Another one of my dreams for the ranch was to make wine there and who better but a Frenchman to take charge of that? I engaged Monsieur Gascon from Bordeaux for that job and I am convinced he made better wine than any ever vinted in California. But a new law which put all liquor into bond for several years spoiled the sale of the bottles which featured my picture on the label.

There was also a sulphur spring on the property which we intended to develop and a quicksilver mine which we thought we had discovered, but I did not have the time necessary to develop their possibilities and turned over this chore to my manager.

The one drawback of the area was the multitude of rattlesnakes, but soon after putting an advertisement on the ranch house offering a reward of a dollar per head, I found long rows of the detestable vipers laid along the front fence, ticketed with the names of the various heroes who had done them in, so I imagine they were soon considerably diminished. I noticed that many horses bore traces of rattlesnake bites on their fetlocks, but I never heard if it was ever fatal to them.

We had another, and in those parts a more unusual, pest to deal with, though not such a dangerous one as the snakes. Black pigs had been allowed to roam about and had thrived and increased to such an extent that they became as savage as wild boars. There must have been hundreds of them and they wrought such havoc to the corn that the cowpunchers had to be commandeered to deal with them, which they did by means of a lasso, and for that they got to keep the pig as well as a dollar reward for each.

I now confess the truth to a rumor that has been prevalent for many years. Yes, Freddie Gebhard was with us on our visit to the ranch. And, yes, Freddie did purchase the adjoining property, on which he built a very utilitarian lodge some few hundred yards from my ranch house. But we did not escape to the ranch for hidden "trysts" at unannounced intervals, as has been so widely rumored. The fact is that circumstances beyond my control prevented me from enjoying my ranch as much I had hoped I would.

While I owned the property for some years, I only visited it one time, for a fortnight, I am sad to say. The following two summers after I purchased the property my work required me to be in London. Finally, I made plans to visit the ranch once again, where my brother and sister-in-law had preceeded us. While we were on our way there a most unfortunate railway accident changed our plans.

Still convinced that the ranch would breed superlative racing stock, I had invested largely in some thoroughbred mares that had been good winners at Monmouth Park, Saratoga, Long Branch and other Eastern race courses. While being shipped West, the train on which they travelled was derailed and fell down a steep slope. Luckily there was no loss of human life, though many passengers were injured, among them the groom in charge.

I rushed to the scene of the accident and was glad to find that I could be useful to the overworked doctors by helping to nurse the injured, but I was so disheartened by the accident that I canceled my visit to the ranch and we all sailed for England instead. I continued to own the property for several years afterwards, but finally sold it for about half the price I paid for it.

Was the ranch my paradise lost? Perhaps. But fate decreed I was to see it only that one time. I often think of "Langtry Farms" and what might have been.

2

A Doctor Named Bethenia

The trip to Portland, at least so I thought, would be uneventful. Little did I realize how wrong I was.

I asked Beverly if he was sure the new costumes by Worth that had just arrived from London were carefully packed. I was, of course, unduly concerned — Beverly was too efficient to overlook something as important as my new costumes. He advised me in his very proper manner that not only were they carefully packed — separate from the older costumes — but he had also made sure they would not wrinkle in order for them to be ready for our opening in Portland on Friday.

The scenery throughout Northern California was stunningly beautiful. The redwood trees were bigger than any I had ever seen and I needed little convincing that some trunks had been carved out to be wide enough to drive a stage through without touching either side. Southern Oregon was equally beautiful and I was looking forward to my first visit to the area with great anticipation.

As our trip North progressed on the Lalee I began to feel a discomfort in my head. It seemed like the beginnings of a head cold — the bane of any actress — and then the symptoms were all too similar to when I had been temporarily felled by typhoid some years ago. Freddie noticed I wasn't my usual self, whatever that might mean, and I told him it was nothing. He wouldn't accept my excuse, however, and when he touched my forehead he then knew I was burning with a fever.

Since there was no doctor aboard there was not much we could do other than apply cold compresses, using the ice from the large chest that we had packed at the ranch. It helped relieve the discomfort a bit, but it was obvious my fever was not subsiding. Freddie insisted we stop at Roseburg, the next town, and seek out a doctor. I was in no condition to object for two reasons. One, I was not feeling well at all and secondly, I did not want to disappoint my fans in Portland by canceling our opening.

Freddie set out to find a doctor. To his consternation, he was first told there was none in town. He would have to wait for our arrival in Portland, several miles to the North, to find one. Then, a local woman took him aside and told him there really was a doctor in town — it's just that she was a *woman* and the men resented the fact so much that they would not even acknowledge she was practicing medicine in their town. Freddie was desperate. He sought out this woman doctor and brought her to me.

Her name was Bethenia Angelina Owens or, more properly put, *Doctor* Bethenia Angelina Owens. While not what I would call pretty, she had a pleasant enough face and, more importantly, the self-confidence all good doctors need. Why the male citizens of Roseburg resented a woman doctor so much puzzled me, so while she was treating my fever I asked her to tell me a little about herself.

It seemed that Bethenia Owens was at her best when the odds were against her. Some called it courage, some called it determination — while others even called it stupidity —

but no matter what her motivation, she was a woman of destiny who was certainly ahead of her times.

Bethenia was only three years old in 1843 when she crossed the plains from Missouri in a covered wagon with her father and mother, Thomas and Sarah Damron Owens. The family settled in Clatsop County in Northwestern Oregon, where Thomas established a farm near the mouth of the Columbia River.

Though slight of build, Bethenia was a tom-boy out of necessity. She could ride horseback and shoot equally as well as her brothers, but her main duties as a child were helping her mother with the children — there were nine in all. "I was the family nurse and it was seldom that I had not a child in my arms," she told me. But her chores didn't prevent her from rough-housing with her brothers and more than holding her own (this reminded me much of my own youth in Jersey with my five brothers). Bethenia once won a bet from her siblings that she could carry four sacks of flour weighing a total of two hundred pounds as far as they could.

She saw no reason women could not be the equal of men (amen!), a philosophy she expounded even as a youngster and which was to guide her the rest of her days. She said, "I realized very early in life that a girl was hampered and hemmed in on all sides simply by the accident of sex."

But Bethenia was never convinced she was a member of the "weaker sex." When she was just ten years old the renegade Indian "Spuckem" robbed the farm while the senior Owens was away and harassed Bethenia, her mother and the other children until their father returned home and drove him off the property. Word soon got back to the Owens from friendly Indians that Spuckem had sworn vengeance against the Owens and would return and kill them. And return he did. Alone in the house at the time, Bethenia fought him off until her father returned and wrestled the Indian's gun away from him and killed him. Bethenia wrote years later, "Thomas Owens was not afraid of man nor devil." Neither, I might add, was Thomas Owens' plucky daughter.

Getting an education was not an easy task for Bethenia. She was twelve before she had any formal schooling. Her teacher was a handsome young man by the name of Beaufort and by the time her three-month term was over and Beaufort was ready to move on, Bethenia was in love. Beaufort chidingly told her mother, "I guess I'll take this one with me," and when Bethenia ran down the road hoping that he would, he gently told her the most important thing in her young life was to study hard and make something of herself — advice Bethenia never forgot. Later, whenever she was especially rebellious, which was not infrequently, her brothers and sisters would say, "I wish the teacher had taken you with him," to which Bethenia never failed to reply, "I wish he had, too!"

When she was fourteen, Bethenia married Legrand Hill, who turned out to be a ne'er-do-well who failed at whatever he tried, from farming to a brick manufacturing business. And, despite the fact that Bethenia's father, now a successful farmer, constantly bailed them out of the financial doldrums Hill encountered, the marriage was doomed to failure. Hill was not only a poor provider, he was a wife beater as well and this Bethenia would not tolerate. So, despite being severely admonished by a neighbor that adultery — something, with all his shortcomings, Hill was not guilty of — was the only grounds for divorce, Bethenia took their two-year-old child, George, and left her husband. After winning her divorce decree in court, Bethenia petitioned for the restoration of her maiden name and vowed never again to go by any other last name than Owens. Later, she gained no small satisfaction when her neighbor's own daughter left her husband, who also was a wife beater, and the woman publicly apologized to Bethenia.

It was now 1858 and Bethenia was an eighteen-year-old divorced mother with little formal education. But she considered herself an adult with all the attendant responsibilities and she was determined to support herself and her infant son with no outside help. Much to the chagrin of her family she was not above taking in washing, ironing and sewing, picking berries and doing some nursing (more like housekeeping in those days) to earn a living. She also returned to school, and friends recall seeing her ironing and reading at the same time.

By 1861 Bethenia had progressed enough to begin teaching, albeit oftentimes she was barely ahead of her students while preparing her lesson plans. One thing she was well-prepared for, however, was any disciplinary action that had to be taken. There was one seventeen-year-old boy in particular who continued to disrupt her class until she forced him to stay after school. He reacted by failing to come to school the next day, upon which Bethenia collared the boy in the street and in no uncertain terms made him go to class. Her reward was a vicious kick from his heavy boot, after which Bethenia seized the boy and adeptly threw him to the floor. She said, "He had not expected to encounter such muscle in a lady," and he was no trouble after that. In fact, he quickly spread the word, "It's no use fooling with that teacher. She don't scare worth a cent!"

Bethenia now had a steady income and the security of a small cottage in Astoria which she purchased with her earnings. But someone out of her past was soon to return.

14

Bethenia's errant ex-husband, Legrand Hill, reappeared and asked her to remarry him. But, as she told me, "He had not found the young, ignorant, inexperienced child-mother whom he had neglected and misused, but a full-grown, self-reliant woman who could look upon him only with pity." The rebuffed Hill was never heard from again.

Shortly thereafter, Captain A. C. Farnsworth, a middle-aged bachelor and river bar pilot, made her a no-strings-attached offer of enough money to attend any school in the U.S., but Bethenia turned him down, preferring to make it on her own rather than being obligated to anyone. As she said, "The acceptance of that offer would doubtless have changed my life, but who can tell if for better or worse?" There were times, however, when she admitted she regretted not accepting the generous offer from Capt. Farnsworth.

After spending some time as a teacher, Bethenia decided to move to Roseburg, Oregon, where her parents now lived. The trip, according to Bethenia, was reasonably uneventful other than the fact that she and her young son were attacked in a storm by a band of roving, wild and ravenous wolves!

In Roseburg, she opened a dress and millinery shop, where she prospered for two years. Then, a new and more experienced milliner moved right next door and Bethenia was faced with competition from a strong challenger. But it was when the odds were against her that Bethenia functioned at her best. She went to San Francisco to study under the professional milliners there and, with her newly acquired knowledge — plus some tips she surreptitiously gained from her next-door competitor — she showed a tidy $1500 profit after her first year back.

Bethenia's difficult times seemingly were behind her. A lesser woman might have decided to live a quiet life, but not Bethenia. It was at this juncture that she decided to go against the odds once again or, in her own words, "climb a slippery ladder," and become a doctor.

The year was 1870 and the incident that prompted Bethenia's newest adventure was when she was at a friend's house and, because of her experience in nursing, was asked to attend to a sick child until the doctor arrived. The physician, who turned out to be old and bumbling, did more harm than good as he repeatedly was unsuccessful in attempts to lance the child's infected arm. Finally, an exasperated Bethenia grabbed the scalpel and made the incision, finally bringing the small patient some relief. It was this incident that convinced Bethenia, who was not thirty, that her true calling in life was to be a doctor. She called on a physician friend, a Dr. Hamilton, and borrowed all the medical books he would lend her. The Hon. S. F. Chadwick, upon learning of her interest in medicine, gave her the only encouragement she would receive: "Go ahead. It is in you; let it come out. You will win," he told her.

There was no additional encouragement for Bethenia to enter medicine. It was a field almost totally restricted to males, especially in the West. Even her own family was aghast that she would entertain the thought of going to medical school and her father and brothers did their best to discourage her. They felt the barriers were too great even for the strong-willed Bethenia. Even women rallied against her and one of her best female friends accused her of having lost her senses. "You're a good milliner, but I'll never have a woman doctor about me!" she not-so-politely informed Bethenia.

The criticism did not deter her. She went to Philadelphia and enrolled in the only school that would have her because she was a woman, the Eclectic School. Realizing the school's reputation was suspect, Bethenia employed a private tutor from one of the better medical schools to assist her studies toward a degree.

Shortly after her graduation, Bethenia stopped home in Roseburg on her way to Portland, where she had decided to practice. The medical community in Roseburg was so opposed to female physicians that they decided to put Bethenia in her place. She was invited to an autopsy on the supposition she would demur. But the good doctors should have known better and Dr. Bethenia Owens eagerly accepted the invitation.

Some half a hundred spectators stood outside the small shed as Bethenia entered, accompanied by the town's five male doctors. As she took her place, a Dr. Palmer announced, "I object to a woman being present at a male autopsy, and if she is allowed to remain, I shall retire!"

To which Bethenia replied, "I came here by written invitation and I will leave it to a vote whether I go or stay, but I would like to ask Dr. Palmer what is the difference between the attendance of a woman at a male autopsy and the attendance of a man at a female autopsy?"

Dr. Palmer did not have an answer and when his colleagues voted to allow Bethenia to stay, he stormed out. The remaining physicians were not finished with Bethenia, however. As one of them picked up his scalpel, he offered it to Bethenia. Surprised, she said, "You do not want me to do the work, do you?" He smiled and nodded. Bethenia took the instrument and, as the shocked doctors looked on, lit a cigar — it was the custom at autopsies in those days to drown out the stench of the corpse — and then she proceeded to make the first incision.

While she worked, the word of the amazing incident raced through town and hundreds more gathered outside. But instead of welcoming a new doctor to their town, the citizens of Roseburg greeted Bethenia with jeers and catcalls, and if her brothers had not been in town to protect her there's no telling what might have happened. (Obviously, as Freddie found out, there is still an element in town that resents a female physician.)

Bethenia quickly departed for the more civilized environment of Portland, opened her office and specialized in treating women and children. Her practice was progressing well enough to earn her enough money to send her son, George, to medical school at Willamette University in Oregon, to finance her sister's college education and to take in Mattie, the daughter of a deceased patient whom she adopted and also sent to medical school.

During this period, while traveling between Portland and Roseburg, Bethenia's stage was delayed by a bank robbery at a rest stop in a small village. The local sheriff had been seriously wounded by a gunman who was holed-up in the bank and she was the only doctor available. She treated the sheriff and saved his life, but while she was finishing up, the gunman attempted to make his escape. Bethenia calmly took the sheriff's gun, took careful aim, and wounded the gunman enough to stop him. She then tended to his wounds, proclaiming that a doctor's duty is to heal the sick — no matter who it might be.

On another occasion, Bethenia learned of a seriously ailing young prostitute in a local house of ill repute who was being denied medical attention. Forsaking her usual conservative attire, she dressed as a "lady of the evening," carefully concealed her medical bag, and gained entrance to the brothel, where she attended to the gravely ill girl and saw to it that she was returned home to her family.

Bethenia was to be faced with a major crisis before too long when it was learned (many believe her nemesis, Dr. Palmer, was behind this) the college in Philadelphia from which she had earned her medical degree had been accused of selling fraudulent credentials. There were rumors, fanned by Dr. Palmer, that Bethenia was not a legitimate doctor at all and she should be forced to close her practice. Bethenia decided to dispel the rumors once and for all by enrolling in the prestigious and nationally renowned Jefferson Medical College in Philadelphia. But the barriers against women doctors were strong, and the school was resolute in its opposition to enrolling female medical students. Even the then-greatest surgeon in the U.S., Professor Gross, could not convince his colleagues to accept Bethenia at Jefferson, so on his advice she then enrolled at the University of Michigan Medical School, which was co-educational and among the top schools in the country.

Studying day and night — Bethenia was a regular four a.m. riser even in her youth — and on semester breaks, she earned her degree in less than half the normal time. Then it was on to Chicago for residency work, where she was joined by her son, now Dr. George Hill, after which they took a tour of Europe to study new techniques. Upon returning to the U.S., an incident at the Customs Office reminded Bethenia that she was still a maverick. The Customs officer took several hours before he would let her take some medical instruments she had purchased overseas into the U.S., never quite believing that a woman could be a doctor!

In 1884, Bethenia married Col. John Adair, a man she knew as a teenager, and whom she admits she "admired and was quite fascinated with even then." She was now forty-four and, true to her vow to never give up her maiden name, she became Dr. Bethenia Owens-Adair. At forty-seven, she gave birth to a child who died just three days afterwards.

I never saw Bethenia again after she treated — and cured me, I might add — that night. But I learned through correspondence that she continued to practice for eleven years after moving to a farm at the insistence of her husband. She then returned to Portland to take up a more active practice and became an enthusiastic lecturer and writer on health subjects and strongly pointed out the importance of exercise for good health, especially among women. When I told Bethenia that I jogged two miles each and every morning, she highly applauded my regimen and assured me it would do wonders for not only my health, but my figure as well. She was a firm believer in temperance (I did not tell her I sipped champagne on occasion) and wrote and lectured on the debilitating effect alcohol had on good health. And, of course, she was continually a strong supporter of the women's suffrage movement.

Bethenia finally retired in 1905, but she still found time to mount her favorite horse and collect some bad debts. It was during her rounds at this time that she was attacked by a crazed murderer whom she promptly captured while armed with only a buggy whip. She may have been in her sixties, but she was still agile and strong!

They honored Bethenia in Portland soon after her retirement and she must have marvelled at the changes in society that she had seen and been a part of. As a child she had crossed the nation in a covered wagon. Now the automobile was on the scene as well as the electric light, the telephone and even the airplane. It was an exciting era — I can attest to that!

Bethenia told her audience, "In this day and age of progress and plenty, women are found in all pursuits of life, from the cradle to the grave, and it is hard now, and will be more so, for women a century hence, to believe what their privileges have cost their early mothers in tears, anguish, and contumely, as they ascended, step by step, that slippery and dangerous highway, clinging courageously to the rope and tackle of progress, taking in the slack here and there, never flinching, and never turning back."

As I think about my encounter with this fascinating and wonderful woman, I often remember they called Bethenia "the woman who dared." How right they were!

3

The Spy Sisters

My travels throughout America brought me into contact with many unforgettable characters — some famous, some not. The Moon sisters rank among the most unforgettable of all.

I feel I have always been a woman who is just a bit out of step with her times, yet, by the very fact that I am, it has seemed to set me apart from my peers. Indeed, it has made me some sort of a celebrity that many of them wish to emulate. I think back to my early days in London society when, while still in mourning for my dear departed brother Reginald, I wore nothing but black for a year and kept my hair in a rather severe and conservative knot. Imagine my surprise when I suddenly saw this style duplicated by other London women who thought my attire and coiffure was significant enough to be a trend-setter.

Then there was the time I first smoked a cigarette in public — shocking, I admit, but soon there were many other women who were as plucky as I in this regard. And when I disrobed down to my underslip in a recent play — something that was demanded by the playwright's manuscript, I should point out — I was chastised by the press (all male, keep in mind) for my supposed immodesty, yet many persons both male and female approached me in private to congratulate me for daring to break long-standing barriers.

Women, I submit, too often are forced to play submissive roles in society because this is a man's world and the men make the rules. But rules that interfere with the progress of the species should be broken and if I have played a small part in this process, I am proud of it. But my role is rather insignificant when I look at the obstacles that many brave women, by dint of their own grit, have overcome. Two of the bravest of these unique women are the magnificent Moon sisters, Ginnie and Lottie.

I had the privilege of meeting both women during a tour of the Southern part of the U.S. We were playing in Memphis, and both sisters came backstage and introduced themselves. At the time, of course, I had no idea who they were other than two admiring members of the audience. But in conversing with them I eventually learned their story, and what a story it was!

The American Civil War ended about a quarter of a century ago, but a great many of the participants are still as vibrant as ever. There is no question that the war was the most significant event in American history, equally as important as the Revolution, when the colonies declared their independence from Mother England.

We are all quite familiar with the now-legendary participants of the Civil War — the great Union president, Abraham Lincoln. General Ulysses S. Grant, with whom I had the pleasure of dining in London some years ago. The South had its famous general Robert E. Lee and the president of the Confederacy, Jefferson Davis. These are but a few of the famous men of the Civil War who will go down in history, never to be forgotten as long as history books are written.

But there were thousands of others, all participants in that great conflict, whose exploits will soon disappear from memory and fade into dust as time continues its inexorable march. The Moon sisters are among that group, and in my own small way, I would like to relate their story here. It deserves to be told — and preserved for future generations.

Ginnie, more formally Virginia, and her sister Lottie (Charlotte), were from the state of Ohio. Ginnie was the younger and prettier, often described as a legitimate beauty. Lottie, fifteen years her senior, was not accorded that accolade, but nevertheless had an undeniable attraction to men as we shall find out. There was another Moon sister in between Ginnie and Lottie, but Mary soon fades from our story because she never took part in the activities that made Ginnie and Lottie special. Because, you see, Ginnie and Lottie were Civil War *spies!*

It was during that great conflict, with the American nation torn asunder, that these two women from the Northern state of Ohio made it plain and clear that they were Southern sympathizers. And they were not about to sit home and sew and wrap bandages as did most of the women of that period. Indeed, they were soon to take an active and most dangerous part in the war.

Ginnie's initial war effort was to get herself engaged to no less than sixteen soldiers at one time. Her logic, she maintained, was quite understandable: "If they'd died in battle, they'd have died happy, wouldn't they? And if they lived, I didn't give a damn."

Lottie's romances were even more significant. She was about to be married to a man who was later to become one of the Union army's most famous officers. While standing at the altar and asked by the minister "Do you take this man as your lawfully wedded husband?," Lottie vigorously shook her head negatively, grabbed her wedding gown and said, "No-siree-bob!" as she made a hasty retreat from the church. The groom who was left standing at the altar was none other than future general and commander of all Union forces, Ambrose Burnside. As it turns out, he would have his chance for sweet revenge in the not too distant future.

Ginnie and Lottie Moon were women right after my own heart. This was America in the middle part of the century, remember, when women knew their place and were expected to stay there. Yet the Moon sisters were not above wearing the widest skirts they could find, topped by flowered headgear. Rather than demurely look away when in the company of the opposite sex, they instead would brazenly flirt with the boys and turned their noses up at custom. They were rebels in their youth and never changed. Ginnie was a veteran cigarette smoker by the 1880s and was not reluctant to sit in church, puffing away, while parishioners looked on in amazement. And to think the minister of the church was Ginnie's own nephew!

Ginnie would have been right at home in the Wild West. She carried a gun most of her life, a pearl-handled revolver, and more importantly, she was a crack shot. In later years she kept the pistol hidden in an umbrella that was forever at her side, and woe be it to anyone who tried to part her from her bumbershoot.

One would think that the sisters had come from a less than exemplary background, but, on the contrary, their family was of high standing and Ginnie and Lottie could be perfect ladies whenever it was necessary. Both were petite, with dark hair. Ginnie, born in 1844, was a beauty with her blue eyes and exquisite features. Lottie, being the older sister by fifteen years, wore her hair in a severe style, and was called "interesting" looking but "the smartest woman in the world."

The girls' affinity for the Southern cause undoubtedly stemmed from the fact that their father, Robert S. Moon, was a native Virginian, tracing his roots back to Colonial days. He has been described as "a reader, a thinker, a man of gentle and tolerant ways." Mrs. Moon, on the other hand, has been called "close-lipped, unbending, an orthodox Presbyterian." An interesting blend from which the Moon sisters evolved.

Lottie became a rather good amateur actress, which was to stand her in good stead when she took up her career as a spy. She also had a unique trick of throwing her jaw out of place with a cracking sound, something she would use to advantage during her upcoming espionage days. She continued her erratic amorous ways before the war, because after she ran out on Ambrose Burnside, she supposedly accepted a marriage offer from not one, but two suitors at the same time. The man she eventually married, attorney and future judge James Clark, shoved a revolver into Lottie's side the day of their marriage and advised her, "There'll be a wedding today or a funeral tomorrow." Lottie became Mrs. Clark with no further ado.

With the advent of the war, the girls' two brothers enlisted in the Confederate army and Mrs. Moon, following the death of her husband, moved to Memphis, Tennessee. Ginnie remained in Ohio where she attended the Oxford Female College, but once the war started she rebelled against the Northern sympathies of the college faculty and demanded she be allowed to join her mother in Memphis. Though only seventeen, she proved her loyalty to the South by taking out her pistol and calmly shooting out every star on the Union flag that waved over the school grounds.

Lottie was the first sister to actually participate in an act of espionage for the Southern cause. Still living in Ohio, but near the Kentucky border, her husband learned that messages from Confederate General Sterling Price had to be taken to General Edmund Kirby-Smith in Kentucky. He was surprised when Lottie volunteered to carry them.

Taking advantage of her acting skills, Lottie dressed as an elderly Irish woman, made her way through the Union lines by using an Irish brogue on the assembled Union troops, the majority of whom were Irish, and after a series of harrowing escapes, completed her mission.

Flushed by that success, Lottie subsequently carried many vital messages to the South. Her next major effort took her to Canada, where she chose the guise of an ill English matron who had crossed the Atlantic for the sole purpose of visiting the hot springs in Virginia — for health purposes. Armed with documents forged by the Confederates, Lottie eventually made her way into the Union capital, Washington, D.C., where she asked none other than Secretary of War Edward Stanton for a pass to cross the lines into Virginia. The ruse worked — at least well enough to get her out of Washington. But when she reached the Shenandoah Valley, Union authorities became suspicious of the "English" lady. General F. J. Milroy listened patiently while she explained that actually she wanted to go to Hot Springs, Arkansas, not Hot Springs, Virginia. She even resorted to using her old "dislocated jaw" trick, explaining it was caused by her arthritic ailment, which was becoming more serious all the while. The general insisted that his own physician examine Lottie and, while not agreeing to let her proceed to Virginia, he did allow her to move on to Cincinnati, Ohio, where she was ultimately to meet up, albeit unexpectedly, with her sister Ginnie.

By now Ginnie had made her way to Memphis, which was still in Confederate hands despite the relentless drive by the Union army to capture the city. Ginnie was not content to help her mother roll bandages and nurse wounded soldiers. She wanted more exciting action. And she got it. Using her feminine wiles, she made her way through the Union lines carrying vital military facts to the beleaguered Confederate forces which were retreating from the Memphis area.

Early in 1863, Ginnie was in Jackson, Mississippi, when she learned that Confederate General Sterling Price had intelligence information he felt was vital to pass on to the Ohio Knights of the Golden Circle, a group of Southern sympathizers. Ginnie, pointing out her Ohio background, volunteered to carry the information. She casually picked up her mother in Memphis and made the trip back to Oxford, Ohio, and accomplished her mission by passing the information on to her brother-in-law, Jim (now Judge) Clark, who saw to it that it got to the Ohio Knights.

The return trip to Memphis, however, would not be so easy. General Ambrose Burnside — the man jilted by Ginnie's sister Lottie some years before — was now head of the Union Department of Ohio and was determined to weed out the "traitors" who lived under his jurisdiction. He issued general orders that said "the habit of declaring sympathies for the enemy will no longer be tolerated" and went so far as to threaten "dire punishment for all who aided the rebellion." Little did he know that his former betrothed was one of those who was actively engaged in "aiding the rebellion."

By now Union officials had become suspicious of Judge Clark and planted a counterspy in the Clark household. The young man reported back to his superiors that there were no suspicious goings on in the Clark house, but he was curious over the fact that the ladies "did nothing but quilt day and night."

Ginnie now asked their new friend to help her and her mother get passes to return to Memphis by way of Cincinnati. He was glad to accommodate them and soon Ginnie and her mother were aboard a ship, waiting to leave. But the Union spy was wise to something and had advised the ship's captain not to sail without special orders from the Army.

Ginnie had a secret dispatch from the Knights of the Golden Circle hidden in her bosom. Before the ship could sail, she was arrested by Captain Harrison Rose, a customs official, who claimed she was "an active and dangerous rebel in the employ of the Confederate government who has contraband goods and rebel mail and is the bearer of dispatches."

Captain Rose took Ginnie to her cabin where he said he was under orders to search her. "*You,* a man, ordered to search *me?* I'll never endure it!" Ginnie protested.

He confidently replied, "How can you help it?"

Ginnie had the answer. From a slit in her skirt she took out a Colt revolver, aimed it at his head and said, "If you make a move to touch me, I'll kill you, so help me God!"

Captain Rose hesitated. Obviously, this woman means business, he thought. Playing her best card, Ginnie said, "Does General Burnside know of this? I don't think he does. He has been a friend of mine since I was five. You had better be careful what you do or I will report you to him!"

Stalling for time, Ginnie realized she had the incriminating evidence on her person and must destroy it. Her ruse worked. Captain Rose said he would return, and left, taking her luggage and keys. But while he was gone Ginnie took the papers from her bosom, "dipped them in the water pitcher and in three lumps swallowed them."

When the Captain returned he ordered Ginnie and her mother to be taken to the customs office. There, their luggage was examined and among the items found was a large ball of opium.

The officer in charge asked "What are you doing with that?"

Ginnie did not so much as blink as she replied, "My mother can eat that much in a month. She requires it for health reasons."

Mrs. Moon squirmed a little in her chair, but said nothing. Ginnie, in an attempt to cover for her mother said, "She might be under the influence of it even now."

The official then picked up a quilt, ripped it open and discovered opium, quinine and morphine, all drugs desperately needed by the Confederates. Ginnie's multitudinous petticoats were then examined and according to the next day's newspapers, she had been wearing "forty bottles of morphine, seven pounds of opium and a quantity of camphor."

Ginnie and her mother were put under arrest, but rather than being housed in an all-male prison, they were sent to the Burnet House, whereby Ginnie's erstwhile enemy, Captain Rose, asked her to dinner. Ginnie charmed and humored the Captain by agreeing, saying "You are my jailer. I suppose I have to put up with you."

Ginnie learned that General Burnside was in town and she soon had an audience with him. She explained to him, not really knowing what his feelings would be toward her considering the desertion of Burnside by her sister Lottie at the altar plus the fact both women were now spies for the enemy, that she was apparently going to be sent away to be tried by General Rosecrans and had no idea what fate was awaiting her.

General Burnside, ever the gallant gentleman, tossed aside any ill feelings he might have harbored, and told her, "Have no fear, my child. I shall try you myself."

Soon thereafter, with his junior officers realizing Ginnie was a friend of the General's, she was being entertained at dinner and even was invited to the theater, which she politely declined, saying she did not want to break the rule which forbad her from leaving the hotel.

Lottie Moon was the next to cross paths with General Burnside. Once again assuming her guise as an English traveler, she had the audacity to appear in front of her former suitor to plead for passage to Virginia, thinking she could fool the man who had courted her only a few years earlier. The bemused General let Lottie play out her part, gently getting a bit of revenge for being jilted by keeping Lottie waiting an agonizingly long time for an answer as he tried to discourage her from further espionage activities. He finally remanded her to the authorities in Cincinnati, where she joined her sister and mother under surveillance, albeit the punishment was less than severe.

The great war ended with no action being taken against the Moon sisters even though it was no secret to victorious Union officials that they had been active espionage agents for the South right up to the end. Ginnie was taken into custody for a time but she proved to be such a nuisance that she was eventually allowed to return to Confederate territory.

In relating this story I find it all the more amazing that Ginnie went through most of her wartime adventures while still in her teens. When the war ended she had just entered into her twenties. After the great conflict she lived for a while in Memphis, as feisty as ever, and eventually ran a boarding house which was limited to men only. The last word heard from her was that she was going to Los Angeles, California, to try her hand at acting in motion pictures.

Lottie became a writer, working both as a novelist and journalist and covered the European capitals during the Franco-Prussian war.

To say that Ginnie and Lottie Moon are two of the most fascinating persons I have ever met is putting it mildly.

It is said that once, while in New York long after the war had ended, while passing Grant's tomb, Ginnie, true to the Southern cause to the end, said, "Damn him!" That pretty much sums up the indomitable Moon sisters.

4

The Mystery of
Lola Montez

I record the following not only because it is an interesting chapter in my life, but also because it is one of the most mysterious.

The knock on my dressing room door was faint and delicate, definitely not the pounding I had become accustomed to from the cowboys, miners and other male admirers who generally would attempt to see me following a performance in Western America. While my maid, Dominique, was usually adept enough to dissuade the men from proceeding much beyond the doorway, there was a burly local policeman usually within calling distance should we need assistance which, I am happy to report, was not often. The cowboys, despite being a rather rough-hewn lot, were usually gentlemen enough when politely asked to leave.

This gentle knock, however, piqued my curiosity, and as Dominique approached the door I turned from removing my makeup to see who might be there. It was a woman, as I had suspected, and I nodded to Dominique to let her in.

She was, I would guess, in her late thirties to early forties, but far be it from me to try to guess the age of a lady approaching her middle years. Her dress was what the local ladies call their "Sunday best," black, conservative, and certainly not flattering. She was carrying a black valise, which I thought a bit unusual, but she looked harmless and even somewhat frail, although the dark ringlets of hair that framed her face indicated she could be rather pretty given the proper attention. She hesitated in approaching me and I could see she was timid and frightened, so I smiled at her and beckoned her toward me.

"Yes," I said, trying to sound friendly, "What can I do for you, madame?"

"Forgive the intrusion, Mrs. Langtry, but might I have a moment of your time?" she replied.

"Please, sit down," I said, indicating the chair near my dressing table. She placed the valise beside the chair as she sat. She hesitated and did not speak.

"Well, now, what is it that brings you here, Miss...?" I asked, attempting to break the tension.

"*Mrs.* Marguerite Madison," she quickly interjected, "I live here in Virginia City and when I heard you were appearing at Piper's, I knew I must see you."

"And did you enjoy the play?"

"Yes, very much," she said, "but I meant I must see *you* — talk to you."

"Oh?"

"I have something to tell you that I've told no one else in the world. Not even my husband. But it is a story you will understand — I just know you will."

"Well, Mrs. Madison..."

"Marguerite...please call me Marguerite."

34

"Very well," I continued, "you will forgive me if I remove my make-up while listening, but I promise you have my rapt attention."

Marguerite fidgeted for a moment, slightly embarrassed. Then she drew a breath and began her story.

She asked me if I had ever heard of Lola Montez and I nodded affirmatively. I had, in fact, been compared to Lola Montez by an English journalist who, I suspect, was searching for a story to fill the columns of his somewhat less than reputable gazette. Marguerite was obviously very knowledgeable of the late actress and I admit to being curious about what she had to say about her.

She told me that Lola Montez, despite her very Spanish-sounding name, was born in Limerick, Ireland, in 1818, the daughter of an officer in the Royal Navy, Ensign Edward Gilbert. Her mother, Oliverres de Montalva, claimed to be from Spain, though some detractors seriously doubt her veracity. They quickly point out that many modern-day Irish are descendants of Spanish sailors from the Armada who settled in Britain and passed on their olive complexions to their progeny who live even this day. In fact, in a less romantic report, the first name of Lola's mother actually was Elizabeth, although it is acknowledged she might truly have been of Spanish descent. Suffice it to say that Lola's exotic looks certainly indicate she could well have had Spanish blood flowing through her veins.

Lola's given name was Maria Dolores Eliza Rosanna Gilbert, again confirming the strong possibility of her claimed Spanish heritage. And while it is generally conceded that she was born in Ireland, Lola at different times gave her birthplace as Constantinople, Madrid, Lucerne and Calcutta. She encouraged the rumors that she was the daughter of the poet Lord Byron, or that her father was a high ranking Spanish naval officer and that she had been kidnapped and raised by gypsies. The lady was a marvel at manipulating the gullible journalists of her day, relishing in the large amount of space her stories commanded. All of which, to be sure, added to her ability to draw large audiences to her performances. If this is one of the parallels in Lola's life with my own, I plead guilty with a bow to the lady for being not only beautiful but an astute business-woman as well.

The truth of Lola's youth seems to be that she was taken by her family to Calcutta, (one of her supposed places of birth, you will recall) India, in 1822, when her father was assigned to a military post there. Unfortunately, Ensign Gilbert contracted a deadly case of cholera not long after arriving in India, and Lola's mother soon found herself a young widow with an infant daughter in this remote out-post. Mrs. Gilbert remarried in 1824 and soon thereafter deemed it best to send Lola back to England, where she would be raised by relatives and receive a proper education.

By the time she was eighteen, fate would have it that Lola would return to India. A family-arranged marriage to a man some forty-two years her senior, Sir Abraham Lum-ley, a judge of the supreme court of England, was not of her choice nor liking. She quickly eloped with a much younger man, Lt. Thomas James, who was, like Lola's father, as-signed to a military post in India.

The marriage was not a success. Lt. James soon strayed into the bedroom of another woman and Lola left for England. On board the ship which was taking her home, she had an affair with a handsome army captain and became his mistress. Lt. James then took her to court, charging her with adultery — why is it the woman always gets the blame? — and Lola was thereafter shunned by both family and friends.

It was following this distasteful incident that she decided she would have to begin a career that would, if nothing else, earn her a living. Those friends still loyal to her suggested that she transpose her grace on the dance floor to the stage and that she become a professional dancer. Lola became intrigued by the idea and even went so far as to study dancing in Madrid. It was during this period that she changed her name and became "Lola Montez." While the critics were less than impressed by her dancing abilities, she performed in London and then in other major European cities where her beauty overcame whatever shortcomings she might have had as a dancer. (A road I admit I, too, have trod.)

She soon had a loyal following of wealthy admirers who were eager to present her with gifts ranging from precious jewels to estates in their respective countries. Her appearance in St. Petersburg resulted in her becoming a favorite of Czar Nicholas I.

Lola's life was now filled with notables from the upper strata of society and the arts. (Another parallel to my own career — or simply the inevitable result of becoming a popular entertainer? Who can say?) The famous musician Franz Liszt and Lola had a torrid but short-lived romance. Another brief affair was with the writer Alexander Dumas, whose *The Count of Monte Cristo* was the rage of book readers throughout the continent. Her liaison with the journalist Henri Dujarier seemed destined for a longer run than previous ones as he and Lola were sharing living quarters only a matter of days after they first met. But tragedy interrupted this tryst as Dujarier lost his life in a duel.

Lola was now ready and eager for bigger and better conquests. She engineered a meeting with King Ludwig I of Bavaria and, as with previous liaisons, she was soon the favorite mistress of the man whose grandson, Ludwig II, became well-known as the "Mad King."

Her influence over the smitten monarch was quick and thorough. Soon she was advising him on all sorts of matters of state, to the point where it aroused the ire of the populace which threatened to revolt against Ludwig. The king bowed to public pressure and banished Lola from the kingdom, but not before rewarding her with a title. She left Bavaria as the Countess of Landsfeld and Ludwig abdicated the throne in favor of his son just a few weeks after Lola's departure for England.

In 1849 Lola married Cornet George Trafford Heald, another military man, but she was ultimately arrested for bigamy. Lola, thinking she was divorced from Thomas James was, in fact, only officially separated from him. She forfeited her bail and went to Paris. Still a young woman in her early thirties, Lola was determined to resume her career on the stage and when she learned that Heald had been killed in an accident, she set out in earnest on a tour that garnered her surprisingly good reviews.

In 1851 Lola was contacted by the famous American promoter Phineas T. Barnum, who wanted to bring her to the United States. But while agreeable to the idea of touring the U.S., Lola opted not to do it under the aegis of P. T. Barnum, instead signing with Edward Willis to manage her performances in America.

Her debut in New York City was met with poor reviews (thus she preceded me as a European actress not to enjoy good notices from the volatile New York press) and the explosive Lola soon was at odds not only with the press but with her landlord as well, purportedly leaving her lodgings without paying the bill. Yet she continued to tour, playing in major Eastern and Southern cities and then heading West to San Francisco.

It was 1853. Californians were eager and anxious to see the spirited Lola Montez perform. Word of her coming West spread among the many gold camps, and crowds pushed and shoved at every stop to get a glimpse of the famous Lola Montez as she debarked. The Western press, mesmerized by Lola as much if not more than were the European journals, was agog over her tour. The San Francisco Herald reported, "This distinguished wonder, this world-bewildering puzzle, Countess of Landsfeld, has come to San Francisco and her coming has acted like the application of fire to combustible matter. She sways hearts and potentates and editors and public opinion."

Lola's performances in California were met with mixed reactions from her audiences. Yet, the crowds continued to come. It was felt that any shortcomings she may have had as an actress were more than made up by a mere glance at this exotic and exciting beauty. (I have heard this comment from many of my critics, although I fail to see how beauty alone can attract a paying audience. There must be more than a shred of talent lest the audiences would soon cease coming — in my opinion. To make my point I note that the demand for ticket's to see Lola in *School for Scandal* was so great that the best seats sold for sixty-five dollars each!)

It was on her American tour that Lola did her famous "Spider Dance." Often shocking her audiences because of the sensuality of the performance, Lola emulated a Spanish dancer in both costume and technique. She moved upon the stage as if she was being entangled in a giant spider's web. Then, with the dance becoming more torrid, Lola pretended to discover spiders about her clothing and body and shaking and writhing, she would rustle her skirts to reveal her multi-colored petticoats while cleverly maneuvering the cork "spiders" to the floor until she could stomp on them in the classic "tarantella" style. Not surprisingly, it was said she copied the dance from Fanny Elssler's "Tarantule," but Lola gave it a personality all her own and it became the keystone of her repertoire. It was not a rare occasion for Lola to enliven a listless audience with her famed "Spider Dance."

It is interesting to note how shipboard romances played a major role in Lola's life. It was while returning to England from India that she met Heald, whom she eventually married. While crossing the Isthmus of Panama she met American newspaperman Patrick Hull, fell in love, and eventually married him in San Francisco.

They honeymooned in Monterey, then spent much time in the Sacramento Valley, whose beauty I certainly can vouch for. While touring the mining camps, Lola and Hull were impressed with the town of Grass Valley. They built a home there and Lola was content with her days in the small village away from the hustle and bustle of the theater. But Hull missed his newspaper activities and turmoil once again entered Lola's life. Hull became a heavy drinker and in a few months he died of alcoholism.

Lola returned to her performing career, mostly in the area near where she lived and sometimes at makeshift theaters which were a far cry from those she had played in the major cities of the world. But she was enjoying her somewhat benign lifestyle and in Grass Valley she met the mother of Lotta Crabtree and befriended and made a protege of young Lotta, who would become one of the most popular performers on the American circuit in a short while to come.

Lola resumed her career in earnest in 1855 when she went to Australia, but upon her return to the United States she realized her star was descending so she retired to her home in Grass Valley. By 1858 she had taken up the cause of women's rights and went on a lecture tour where she gave advice on beauty, chastised men in general while at the same time defending her somewhat tarnished image.

She now decided to settle in New York and it was there, at the age of forty, that she converted to Methodism. Her funds were diminished, and her health was failing. The world-famous beauty, though still a relatively young woman, was near the end of her turbulent life. But she had lived as full a life as anyone could ever imagine. Dancer, actress, courtesan, friend of artists and royalty, Lola Montez died quietly on January 17, 1861 and is buried in Greenwood Cemetery in New York.

Marguerite was silent for a moment. Then she took what appeared to be a manuscript out of the valise at her side and showed it to me.

It was Lola Montez' story, as Marguerite had told it to me. Written in Lola's own hand, according to Marguerite.

"But Marguerite," I said. "How did you come to possess this manuscript?"

Marguerite smiled. "How I obtained the manuscript is not important," she said. "Let us just say that the truth would only add to the mystery of Lola Montez."

The confusion on my face was readily apparent.

"Do not fret," she said. "The lesson to be learned is no matter how high your star rises, it will ultimately fall. I'm sure you have seen the parallels between Lola's career and your own. Do not make the mistake of Lola Montez and be ill-prepared for the days when you are no longer in the public's favor."

Marguerite stood up. "I must go now, Mrs. Langtry. Thank you so much for indulging me." She turned to leave, then stopped and reached for something in the valise.

"I would like you to have this."

Almost unconsciously I took the item, embraced Marguerite, and before I could say anything else, she was gone.

I looked at what she had put in my hand. It was an exquisite gold comb. It was engraved, "To Lola with love and devotion. Ludwig."

I never saw Marguerite again, but I will never forget those soulful brown eyes and, more importantly, the advice she gave to me. I vowed from that day forward to use my money wisely and to make it multiply.

5

Daughter of the Assassin

Truth, as the adage goes, is stranger than fiction. But where and more importantly, how, does one draw the line between the two?

It had always been my practice to bring my entire company with me whenever and wherever I toured, and this included my visits to the United States. It was, I felt, much easier to work with actors and actresses with whom I was familiar, and vice versa. Additionally, it was smart business, because having my own company gave me the control, if you will, over salaries, production costs and the other myriad things that are necessary to take a show on the road.

Now having made my point about maintaining my own company of actors, let me tell you that I was flexible enough to allow exceptions to the rule. On occasion we would do a performance whereby we would need extra actors or we might become shorthanded because of illness or some other reason. It was always my desire to fill these sometimes unexpected and unplanned vacancies with local performers. Not only did it give some budding young actors and actresses a chance to appear on the professional stage, it was also good business to announce to the local press that a hometown favorite was to appear with Lillie Langtry on a given night.

It was this circumstance that led me to the chance meeting with a young actress whom I shall never forget.

We were in the California border city of San Diego, just a few miles North of Mexico, on a whirlwind tour that had started in San Francisco and had taken us to several California locations I had never before visited, including Santa Barbara, Los Angeles and now, the state's Southernmost city.

Our play was *She Stoops to Conquer,* and our regular actress in the part of "Miss Neville," Kate Hodson, had taken ill with a stomach ailment that seemed determined to hang on for several days. So I decided to use a local performer to fill the part. An item in the San Diego newspaper to that effect resulted in several young ladies coming to audition for the role.

It was not a particularly demanding part and I was not going to be too particular over whom I chose for it. That is, until I cast my eyes on a slender and graceful raven-tressed young woman of about twenty-five years. She stood out from the rest so brilliantly it made it easy for me to select her. And when she recited some lines from Shakespeare, I knew this was more than just a local resident who was having a fling at acting.

I called her forward. "What is your name, miss?" I inquired.

She hesitated for an instant, which I thought was strange, then she replied, "Ogarita...but I use Rita for the stage. Rita...Wilkes."

I smiled and nodded. "Well, Rita, you are obviously a well-trained actress and certainly not a novice at this business."

"Thank you, Mrs. Langtry," she replied. "I am in fact a professional and am on tour in California with the George C. Miln Shakespearean Company of New York."

"Indeed?" I said, arching a curious eyebrow.

"My company has finished its run here in San Diego but we will not be leaving the city for a few days. I would very much welcome the opportunity to perform with your cast even though it will be only for one night."

"We feel privileged to have someone with your talent available to us on such short notice," I said, rising and handing her the manuscript to our play. "It is, I'm sorry to say, a very small part..."

"That is of no concern to me," she said. "I have always been of the opinion that in order to be an actor you must *act* no matter how big or small the part."

"Well stated," I told her. "We will rehearse at one p.m. Curtain is at eight p.m. this evening."

"I look forward to working with you, ma'am," she said, and took her leave.

After Harry McCloud, the stage manager, had dismissed the rest of the aspirants, he came up to me with an irritated expression on his corpulent and ruddy face.

"It's none of my business, Mrs. Langtry," he told me, "but do you know anything about that Wilkes woman you just hired?"

I told him I only knew what I had seen — she was obviously an accomplished young actress who seemed quite dedicated to her profession.

He looked around, almost as if he did not want to be overheard. "Does her last name of 'Wilkes' mean anything to you?"

I must have looked at him strangely, because he quickly added, "'Course not, you being English and all. Maybe it's only us Americans who are touchy about the name."

For some reason his attitude raised my hackles, and I retorted, "Mr. McCloud, the name 'Wilkes' happens to be very *English,* if that is of any import to you."

"How about Wilkes *Booth*?" he said, almost with a sneer. "Or more specifically, *John* Wilkes Booth?"

Now, I must admit I am not a great student of American history, and if I may shift from this story for a moment, I would like to clear up an incident that the press has blown completely out of proportion. Some years ago, in London, I was a guest at a dinner party which was given in honor of General Ulysses S. Grant and his wife. The story, as distorted in the press, was that when introduced to General Grant I supposedly asked him what he had done since his Civil War, to which he is said to have replied, "Well, I've served two terms as *president* of the United States, Mrs. Langtry." Now I will admit the exchange took place, or at least something similar to it, but to imply that I did not know that General Grant had been president of the United States was stretching the story a bit too far. My question might not have been phrased in a clear manner, but you must remember I was a young woman in her early twenties at the time who was more than a bit intimidated over meeting this acknowledged American hero. And to General Grant's everlasting credit, when he replied to my question there was a twinkle in his eye and he did it all in good humor.

I repeat this story only because I am constantly amazed at the twists and turns we take along life's unpredictable path. The young woman whom I had just hired for a small part in our play in this rather remote border city in California, apparently had a definite and distinct connection with one of the major incidents in the history of the United States, and one in which General Grant was an integral player.

I looked Mr. McCloud straight in the eye and told him, "Of course I have heard of John Wilkes Booth, but I fail to see what point you are trying to make, sir."

McCloud moved closer to me, so close, in fact, that I could smell his disgusting tobacco breath. (I have had my fill of men who smoke smelly cigars, with Bertie, I'm afraid, being one of the major offenders.) I stepped back, but he would not be dissuaded from pursuing the subject.

"Rumor has it that this Rita Wilkes is the daughter of the assassin!" he said, his eyes squinting in anger.

I must admit I was taken aback by his statement. And, for one of the few times in my life, I was temporarily at a loss for words. Then I blurted out, "That is of no concern of mine. She is a fine actress and that is all I am interested in at this time."

Then I turned and started to make my way toward my dressing room. McCloud just grunted and moved in the opposite direction, thank goodness. The uncouth man was getting on my nerves.

As I started to turn the doorknob to my dressing quarters, a voice came out of the shadows.

"Mrs. Langtry..."

I turned. It was Rita Wilkes, her olive complexion now almost ashen, her hands trembling.

"I couldn't help but overhear what Mr. McCloud told you. I feel I owe you an explanation."

"An explanation is not necessary, my dear," I told her. "Mr. McCloud, I fear, is a man who sometimes lets the brew take command of his senses. And he seems to be a rumor monger, to boot."

Rita was still trembling, but I could see she wanted to talk with me. "Mr. McCloud is a Union army veteran," she told me. "He claims to have been in Washington when...when it happened."

"And because of the coincidence of your last name he believes these dastardly rumors about you that he seems intent on spreading?" I asked.

"They are not rumors," she said, lowering her eyes.

I opened the door to my dressing room and motioned for Rita to enter. She did, relieved that I had asked her in.

"Rita," I told her, "What has happened in the past is something we cannot change. The less we dwell on these things, the better. But I sense whatever is troubling you will not be that easily dismissed."

Rita nodded. "To this day I do not know the entire story. But some of the facts I have lived with all these years lead me to believe I am, indeed, the daughter of John Wilkes Booth, assassin of Abraham Lincoln, president of the United States."

They say confession is good for the soul, and the tale that Rita poured out to me that warm afternoon in San Diego is one from which great novels are written.

John Wilkes Booth was the youngest son of Junius Brutus Booth of Maryland. The elder Booth was the acknowledged leading actor of the American stage in the period preceding the great American Civil War. He was, as I am sorry to admit many actors seem to be, addicted to the bottle and oftentimes was edging over the border of sanity. Nevertheless, he was an outstanding and gifted Shakespearean actor, famous from the New York stage to the mining camps of California and Nevada for his wonderful performances. His sons followed in his footsteps. Edwin, who suffered so terribly after his brother committed his heinous crime, is today probably the highest ranking actor on the American stage. John Wilkes, youngest and most handsome of the Booth sons and the family favorite, soon joined the rest of the Booths on the stage and was making a name for himself as an eminent performer when the United States split apart and soon were engaged in a terrible war. John Wilkes cast his lot with the Confederacy. He became such a zealot that some thought he was as mad as his father. And while he never actually served in the Confederate army, there were those who thought he was, at the very least, a spy for the South. Suffice it to say, he was an active and ardent admirer of the Southern cause.

There is no record of John Wilkes Booth ever having gotten married, let alone siring a daughter (and a son, as I was soon to learn.) However, being extremely handsome and a popular and well-known actor, he was acquainted with an uncountable number of women and it was certainly possible one of them had become his secret wife.

The official record shows, however, that he was unmarried and childless when, on April 14, 1865, he entered the presidential box at Ford's Theater in the capital city of Washington, D.C., and shot and killed President Abraham Lincoln, a tragedy that shall forever haunt all of us who make our living on the stage. An *actor* killed the beloved president of the United States!

Booth, according to the official story, leaped from the box onto the stage, breaking his leg, but nevertheless was able to make a successful escape. Days later, he was trapped in a barn at the Garrett farm in Virginia, where he was shot and killed by a Union army sergeant named Boston Corbett.

Or so the *official* story goes.

Rita Wilkes told me that Booth had been married to her mother, Izola Martha Mills, sometime prior to the war in Richmond, Virginia. They had two children, Rita, or more formally, Ogarita Rosalie, and Harry. Rita's mother was an actress, hence Rita's interest in the profession. And, to add to the intrigue, Rita contends that her father, John Wilkes Booth, was not the man killed in that barn but, instead, made his escape and was alive to this day!

I must admit, being one who spends much of her life "play acting," the drama of an escaped notorious assassin furtively trying to outwit his pursuers was a tempting story to believe, but I am in no position to verify or deny its validity. Rita maintains that Booth made his way to Mexico, but was sometimes in the Western part of the U.S., living, of course, under an assumed name and with an altered identity. She added that oftentimes he would visit her while she was playing in San Diego, it being only a few miles from the Mexican border and I expected at any moment for the infamous John Wilkes Booth to step out of the shadows of the theater and begin reciting some soliloquy from Shakespeare. But my mind was embellishing an already amazing story.

Rita then pulled out a necklace which she had hidden beneath the collar of her dress. She told me it was one her mother had worn. On it was attached a medallion and inside was a small picture cut from a *cartes de visite* of Booth — a most handsome young man, I must say — with what Rita says was a lock of his jet black hair — very similar, I thought, to the color and texture of Rita's own hair.

I had no proper response to Rita's story. And I could see she did not expect one. It was satisfying enough for her to have an attentive listener who would allow her to recite her tale and I confess she kept my rapt attention throughout.

That night Rita was excellent as she performed her part for us and there were occasions when I thought I could detect in the shadows of the theater a man who closely fit the description of her father. Was it my imagination playing tricks with me? Or had the mysterious John Wilkes Booth indeed come to see his daughter perform? In fact, was the reason that Rita took such a small role in our play merely a way for her to secretly rendezvous with her fugitive father? Then again, how could he have known she would appear in our play on such short notice? My questions only prompted additional questions. And as for the man I thought might be Booth, I shall never know the answer, for as quickly as he appeared in the shadows, he disappeared almost as if by magic.

Rita said her goodbyes soon after the final curtain had rung down and before we could attempt any further contact, she was gone into the night. We were off on the Lalee before dawn, heading North for our ultimate destination of San Francisco.

I never saw nor heard from Rita Wilkes again. But after my visits to America I made it a point to have the New York papers sent to me wherever I might be and one evening, while in Brighton, I was reading the April 15, 1892 edition of the New York *World,* and came across an item headlined: "Wilkes Booth's Daughter. Rita Booth, Character Actress and Wife of Albert Henderson Is Dead." Rita was only thirty-two when she died. And she took her amazing story with her.

THE DIARY OF LILLIE LANGTRY

This is the first time I have told anyone Rita's story. Was she indeed the daughter of the assassin? Or was she merely an actress in pursuit of publicity? Perhaps it is best to let future historians make that decision.

6

Oscar,
The Matchless Mine, H.A.W.
and
"Baby Doe" Tabor

Seeing Oscar at the bottom of a mining shaft in Leadville, Colorado, was the last place I would expect to find the man who wore a lily in his lapel while he walked through London.

It took all day for the Lalee to be pulled ten thousand feet up into the Colorado Rockies to a town called Leadville where there is a new Opera House — a theater, one built by a wealthy man who wishes to bring some culture to this remote mining town. I believed we should never be able to go back down the mountain safely. It was so steep that I freely admit going down was a thought that unnerved me more than a little.

Oscar Wilde joined Freddie and me for this trip and that irascible Irishman had been a frivolous character with the miners, but a hero of the arts in the eyes of the man who recently built the new Opera house that bears his name,

Mr. Horace A. W. Tabor. It was, once again, because of Oscar that I looked forward to appearing in a theater that I knew very little about — but found exciting anyway.

Before we alighted from the Lalee however, the town mayor, who was the same man who built the new Opera House, also called hereabouts the *Silver King,* invited us to visit his silver mine. It was called the Matchless Mine. It was from this mine that Mr. Tabor had made most of his wealth, some say as much as one hundred thousand dollars a month.

The first thing Oscar did upon Mr. Tabor's invitation was go down that frightening mine shaft which they called Shaft Number 3. It is supposed to be the driest on Fryer Hill, but Oscar tells me it was "dank and cold and awfully filthy."

Not liking his slouchy clothes — Oscar can be so silly about such things — they put a huge India rubber suit on him.

Beverly tells me Shaft Number 3 is an extremely deep and dreadfully narrow hole dug vertically into the ground. Oscar told me he went down in "a rickety old wooden bucket where I could not be very graceful."

Personally, I refused to go to the mine. Neither would I ever go down that hole, even though Beverly maintained it was as safe as the Lalee. I cannot imagine such a comparison since being swallowed by the ground could not possibly be like sailing across the top of it in my Lalee. Besides, I have felt quite light headed since arriving in Leadville, which I learned today is the highest city in America.

Once at the bottom of the mine, Oscar discovered the miners were prepared with two ceremonies. The first was that he would open a new shaft and they would thereafter call it *The Oscar.* He did so, but told them he would rather have shares in the mine than have it so named. He explained it all to me this way: "I had hoped that in their grand simple way they would have offered me shares in *The Oscar,* but in their artless untutored fashion they did not." Oscar seems to make even the worst events sound poetic.

The second event in the mine involved supper at the bottom of the shaft. The best I can figure out is that the miners found Oscar an event in himself. He told me they were amazed to discover that art and appetite went hand in hand "with absolutely no bounds." As he explained it, "They cheered me when I touched a match to a cigar and puffed so deeply. They applauded when I downed a drink without so much as changing my expression — as though I had never drunk before." I laughed when he told me these things. But I nearly cried when he said they told him that he was a "bully boy with no glass eye." For Oscar that was indeed a man's compliment coming from such rough and harsh, although he insists, real men.

What amazed Oscar mostly was that the first course for supper was whiskey, the second course whiskey and the third course whiskey. "Still," he said, "they insisted upon calling that supper. And," he added, "I did not attempt to dissuade them from that course at all."

This morning's *Rocky Mountain News* reported that Oscar behaved like a lunatic in the mine. I believe the locals simply do not understand his humor. He can be quite bizarre and unconventional at times, but that is Oscar. Anyway, the *Denver Tribune* reported he drank twelve snorters — a fact I am sure — and that the miners voted him to be a perfect gentleman.

When he returned, we went to the local Casino where we found the miners and their girl friends behaving rather raucously. Oscar pointed out the piano player who had a sign on his piano. It read, "Please don't shoot the pianist; he is doing his best."

Oscar thought the sign was a warning that bad art merits the penalty of death, which reminded him of the note he received before coming here. The note explained that everyone in Leadville carried a revolver and that they would be sure to shoot him or his traveling manager — or me, I suppose. Oscar wrote back: "Nothing you could do to my traveling manager would intimidate me."

Oscar lectured to the miners at Tabor's theater about the Florentines — which most of them slept through, but when he read the autobiography of the silversmith Benvenuto Cellini, they awoke. They are, after all, silver miners and Oscar had piqued their interest. They wanted to know why Oscar had not brought Cellini along, and in fact they insisted he go get him.

"But he is dead," Oscar explained. The response from the miners took Oscar's breath away.

"Who shot him?" they asked.

He explained to me afterwards that he was now convinced that for the miners, "The revolver is their book of etiquette."

The next day I began to feel much better, adjusting, I suppose, to the extremely elevated altitude, which it was explained to me by the local citizens, does not have as much oxygen in the air. And although I had a nagging toothache, it was not yet bad enough to slow me.

Beverly insisted that we return to the Matchless Mine and meet Horace Tabor's beauteous wife, Elizabeth Doe, a woman they refer to as "Baby" Doe. She divorced her first husband and came here from Central City and soon she and Horace became inseparable.

One of the local gossips told me that Mr. Tabor had been married to a woman named Augusta prior to his meeting Elizabeth. When he became wealthy he built Augusta a mansion in Denver, but she insisted on living in the servant's quarters. He eventually was spending more time with Elizabeth than he was with his wife and the story goes that he even purchased the Hotel Windsor in Denver to have a place to put up Elizabeth. I can attest to the fact that it is a marvelous hotel, with three hundred rooms, all with fireplaces, and a swimming pool and steam baths among its other accoutrements. Mr. Tabor's marriage of twenty-six years to Augusta ended in divorce and soon thereafter, Elizabeth became the second Mrs. Tabor.

At the mine Elizabeth, Lizzie or "Baby Doe," — take your choice — told me that Mr. Tabor became a millionaire for an investment that came to around seventeen dollars worth of supplies and food to stake two hungry partners. They discovered a silver vein they turned into a mine they called the Little Pittsburgh. After Mr. Tabor sold his share, earning for him about half a million dollars, he sought to buy another mine to call his own. Some men who brokered mines recommended the Matchless, which was an unproven claim. He paid $117,000 for it and then spent another $33,000 to make sure he had a clear title. He immediately hit a vein of silver that has paid out ever since at the rate of about $80,000 to $100,000 per month.

That information was still not enough to get me to go down that hole.

Lizzie told me her maiden name was Elizabeth McCourt and that she was from Oshkosh, Wisconsin. I told her my real name, Charlotte Le Breton, and that I was from the Isle of Jersey, off the English coast. We laughed together, wondering why women must change their names when they marry. Would it not be an interesting world if just the opposite were true?

Lizzie is a marvelous woman who is also very dedicated to her husband and all his wishes. Of course, what woman would not be enamored of such a man? He showers her with gifts, diamonds and love. Nothing seems to be too much for her. Yesterday he gave her a $90,000 diamond necklace for no special reason other than he thought it would look attractive on her.

They also live rather opulently, in surroundings fit for a king. It would seem they spend more money in a month than the Matchless can produce, but possibly not. I do know they seem to spend as if their income is unending.

I detect that Lizzie is not totally happy, though. She is not accepted by Denver high society, a situation that bothers her immensely. Even though she and Horace Tabor were married in Washington D.C. — he was there filling out the last thirty days of a U.S. senator's seat — at what she describes "a sumptuous wedding" — the social butterflies of Colorado continue to spurn her. She was intrigued by stories of my involvement with London high society and said how much she wished she had been accepted in Denver as I had been in London. I explained to her my acceptance in London was one of chance and took place only after Mr. Langtry and I unexpectedly met an old friend of his who managed to get us an invitation to a London society dinner. It is one of those fortuitous turns in my life for which I am grateful.

The pragmatic Lizzie confessed to me that of even greater concern to her than her being snubbed by Denver society is the recent news that silver may be devalued. She told me that she and Horace have spent millions on parties, food, travel and jewelry and other material things. I informed her that I have invested my money in land all over America — in California, Nevada, Illinois and New York — and it seems a man of Mr. Tabor's wealth would do the same. Possibly he knows something about money that I do not but I honestly feel that land investment is a much sounder idea than spending money as freely as did the Tabors.

I had to leave Elizabeth Doe before I learned much more. I had my performance to do at the Tabor Opera House and afterwards I headed toward my next engagement.

For some strange reason, while watching the Colorado scenery pass by on our way to California, I felt fear for Lizzie. I knew deeply inside me that I would probably never see her again. And I was right.

Recently, I was saddened to learn that the Tabors lost all their money, something, I am sorry to say, that does not surprise me. Lizzie had to leave her sumptuous quarters with all the refinery and marvelous furniture and move to a dingy flat of rooms in a rundown boardinghouse. Horace had to take a job as a laborer for three dollars a day. Lizzie was forced to sell or pawn her jewels just to help pay for food and rent.

After a while Horace got a political appointment as Denver's postmaster. It paid about $3,500 a year, barely adequate for their survival. This lasted for slightly more than a year when, unexpectedly, Horace came down with acute appendicitis and died, leaving Lizzie penniless. His last words to his Baby Doe have become famous: "Never let the Matchless go if I die, Baby. It will make millions again once silver comes back."

THE DIARY OF LILLIE LANGTRY

Lizzie — Baby Doe — moved into the Matchless Mine and has lived there ever since. I wish I could visit her, but cannot travel there now. I have written to her, but have received no answer. The poor thing must feel quite put upon and is probably too ashamed to write back.

7

The Bandit Queen

"Women should be soft, sophisticated, delicate." Those were my mother's words. How frightful she would have found some of the ladies of the American West!

My initial reaction to the statement was one of surprise. I immediately responded with a question. "But what is her real name?"

"That."

"Belle Starr? I have always supposed that was a sobriquet."

"So it was. Her birth name was Myra Maybelle Shirley. Her folks called her May. She took Belle from Maybelle and Starr from her second husband."

I suppose I have more than a score of times been the respondent in some colloquy like the above, in regard to my nearly disastrous meeting with the "Bandit Queen," though I do not remember ever adding what I am about to scribe here: that about heart, soul and heaven — and the existence of a rogue within an otherwise beautiful and intelligent woman.

She was born on a quiet farm in Southwest Missouri. Her parents were John and Elizabeth Shirley. Three years later, John Shirley sold his farm, receiving a healthy profit, and moved his family to the town of Carthage, Missouri, where he built the Carthage Hotel. Maybelle's childhood was happy, with a status that only her rich father's wealth could bring her. She was quite pretty as a child but had a red-hot temper, one that drew her into many fights.

Her mother sent her to the Carthage Female Academy where she was to learn to be a gentlewoman, a lady. She proved to be an excellent student in all the subjects from music and languages to arithmetic and writing and later she learned to shoot as straight as any man in the West. She could also play the piano quite well, which I discovered firsthand when she played for me aboard the Lalee.

It was then, during that surprise visit from her, that I learned when the beautiful young, educated lady, Myra Maybelle Shirley, became the Bandit Queen, Belle Starr. When I met her, she was forty and weather worn, her skin crinkled from the years in the blinding Western sun and in the saddle. I shall attempt here to relate the story she told me in her own words.

"I was fourteen. The war between the states had begun. Union troops destroyed Carthage and all my family's land — our house, my father's hotel and other property. My father helped form small bands of guerrillas to beat back the Yankees. My brother Bud joined Quantrill's Raiders."

"I apologize," I said. "Was this the Quantrill who I have read was a bandit? A thief and murderer?"

She flared with anger at me. "He was a good man," she said bitterly. "He led us against the Northerners. I was fourteen when I started with him as a spy. He rode all through Missouri, clearing the country of those damned Yankees. He would grab up the slaves and take them to

Kansas. That was his purpose, and I helped by working as a spy. A scout."

I will tell you now that while we spoke, Miss Starr gripped a six-gun tightly, its barrel aimed at me. We were alone at the time in the Lalee, having been stopped by Miss Starr and I supposed her gang (Beverly had gone to the engine to learn why we stopped — so I made the assumption once she appeared inside the Lalee). I may not have all of this in logical order, since I confess I was rather frightened at the time, but for the most part I know it to be correct. I also remember reading where Quantrill used the war as his excuse to raid and pillage. He would announce that he was there to carry off Negro slaves to Kansas and free them. Unfortunately, his newspaper reputation was more that he took all opportunities to pick up any valuable property which he could "liberate" while doing so. I refrained from exposing my knowledge of this to Miss Starr for obvious reasons and should acknowledge here that the reports I read on Quantrill were all in publications whose loyalties were with the Northern cause.

"He could ride a horse like no other man I ever knew," Belle Starr continued. "Sat a saddle like a magnificent statue. He wore this soft black hat with a glowing gold cord around it so's we'd know him from the others. But he didn't need the cord. We knew him just by his straight up riding. He wore his cavalry boots too with a shirt that had this colorful needlework one of his women folk done for him. Oh, yes," she swooned, "he was a dandy."

I clearly imagined this fourteen-year-old girl falling in love with the leader of the band of outlaws now known to be the most ferocious ever to ride through the American West.

"Over a thousand men rode with Quantrill," she said.

"Did you know any of them?"

"Yes," she answered quickly. "My sweetheart from Carthage, Jim Reed. When Quantrill was driven into Arkansas by the Yankees though, we lost contact until a few years later when I married him. He was my first."

"And what of your brother?" I asked, wondering if he had survived the war.

"I was scouting near Newtonia. I learned that the Union army was going to go to Carthage and capture Bud. They really hated him. But before I could ride back and warn him, Major Eno of the Union army captured me and took me to a farmhouse where he held me. I got away though. I was so angry I sat down at the piano in that house and banged away one tune after the other until it drove him to distraction. He told me to get out of there. I guess he figured he'd held me long enough so's I wouldn't be able to ride to Carthage to warn Jimmy."

"Was he correct?"

She laughed loudly. "Devil's not always right. His men took the road. I cut across the hills. Heck, I rode so hard I jumped streams a mile wide and leaped every fence along the way. When Eno's men got there, guess who greeted them? Me!" She laughed so loud I thought I heard the chandelier in the Lalee ring along with her.

Then she said softly, "They got him next time. Killed him while he tried to get away. He was almost over the fence when they shot him dead." She sighed, lowered the pistol to her lap and added, "My poor daddy and mommy were destroyed by Bud's death. So, they sold the farm, packed up and moved to Texas near Dallas. Town called Sycene."

She went on to tell me that soon the Frank and Jesse James gang along with the Younger brothers, Jim, Cole,

Bob and John stopped by their place. John Shirley greeted them with open arms, although he was a law-abiding man. Still, the gang was from Missouri and had helped fight off the Yankees.

Jim Reed also came by and before long they were married. The two moved in with Miss Starr's parents. Soon she gave birth to a daughter they named Rosie Lee, but Miss Starr called her "Pearl," and it stuck.

"Only, Jim got bored with farm life," she told me. "He started gambling, then he raced horses. Pa thought he spent a lot of time in Indian Territory making friends with them more than he did with his own kind. Too bad."

"Why is that?" I asked.

"I met my second husband there. Sam Starr. He was Tom Starr's son. Tom was Jim's friend. He was a Cherokee. But marrying him came later."

I was taken aback. She threw that news out as though there was nothing to it. I listened intently to the balance of the tale.

"I met him after Jim shot the killers of his brother — in Arkansas. After that Jim was a wanted man, so he picked me and Pearl up and we headed to the Cherokee nation to hide out with his friends. The law couldn't arrest him on Indian land."

She then explained that they moved to California and Los Angeles where she gave birth to a son named James Edward.

"Things went along just fine," she said, "until Jim got himself in trouble with the law again and we had to take off for Texas." (Belle's father gave them some land so they could develop a farm. Instead, they used it to hide horse thieves.)

"Finally the law was breathing down our necks, so we left the kids with my parents and headed back to the Indian lands. Jim couldn't leave things alone. He and his friends robbed a rich farmer and then we had our hands so full of lawmen that Jim headed off alone and I returned to Sycene."

"Is that when you began your own career? I mean the gun you're holding and all?"

She nodded. "I checked into a Dallas hotel for a while but people started calling me the Bandit Queen. I hadn't done anything yet, either. Just rode with my husband."

"What happened to the money Jim stole from the farmer?"

She smiled. "Oh, that. I had it. I spent it, too. In Dallas. Had me a good time. Might as well. Jim and I got unhitched about then. Good old Jim. He found another young girlfriend and rode off with her. He formed his own gang and started robbing trains and stagecoaches. They put a big reward on his head."

I glanced at her gun again, then gazed back into her eyes. "What happened then?"

"A lawman turned me into a widow. In Paris, Texas. A varmint named John Morris tracked Jim into town and then got him to eat with him at an inn. When Jim wasn't looking, Morris shot my Jim dead. He got seventeen hundred dollars for doing it."

After that Belle married Sam Starr and together they claimed a thousand acres of land along the Canadian River — about forty miles west of Fort Smith. They built a house with a kitchen in the back. Pearl joined them and lived with them for a few years.

"I called the place, Younger's Bend. I thought I would live there the rest of my life — in peace and quiet."

Unfortunately, most of her friends were outlaws, so Younger's Bend became a well-known hideout for them.

"You had to ride through a canyon to get there, so we could easily keep an eye out for lawmen. The boys also hid up river in Robber's Cave when they had to." She leaned back into the chair, the pistol still resting easily on her lap and said, "Jesse James was our first guest, but not our last. Too bad I got us into trouble."

"How did you do that?"

"Bought and sold their stolen horses. Law don't look kindly on that sort of dealings."

They took her to Fort Smith and a judge Isaac Parker, known as "the hanging judge" held the trial. They could have received a long prison sentence, but the judge gave them one year or just nine months if they behaved.

"I went to a Michigan prison and the warden liked me, so I ended up teaching his kids to play the piano. Poor Sam ended up busting rocks for nine months. After we got out, I wanted badly to get home, plant crops, take care of my kids. I intended to live a straight life. But nothing seemed to go right. I was accused of doing things I didn't do. Life was made hard by liars. Then Sam got himself shot by Frank West. I had to take care of him. I tried to get him to give himself up for stealing a horse. If he didn't, the Indian police would surely kill him. He agreed. We rode into Fort Smith, me packing two pistols, one on each hip. He was charged, I bailed him out. It was that simple. Then it happened," she said, her voice trailing off.

I searched her eyes with my own, to try to understand, but nothing came. Finally I couldn't wait any longer. "What happened?"

"We was at a dance at a neighbor's house. Frank West came looking for Sam. Sam and him got to arguing about

Frank West shooting my horse out from under Sam when they had their first run in. They backed up, each man going for his gun at the same time. They shot together and — " She stopped speaking, her voice cracking.

"And?"

"They killed each other."

"Oh, my!"

"I loved him. But after that, I had to either leave the farm or marry another Indian. Only Cherokees can own Cherokee farms."

"What did you do?"

"I got Tom Starr's adopted son Bill July, to move in with me. At least for a while that was good enough to hang on to Younger's Bend. I married him recently."

Just then, Miss Starr leaped to her feet, bringing her pistol up as though ready to shoot me. Then she whirled around to face a man who came crashing through the Lalee's door. It was her son, Eddie Reed. Blood flowed from his head.

Miss Starr ran to him and helped him from the Lalee to a wagon that they had brought with them. Before she left, she glanced back to me, bowed her head a little and shook it sadly as though to say, "The troubles continue."

I watched while she got Eddie to the wagon and then she drove off as fast as the two horses could carry them.

I never really understood what she was doing aboard the train, or why they stopped it. I assumed at the time it was to rob the train, but apparently it was due to a man named Mose Perryman who it was that shot Eddie Reed.

The encounter left me breathless and exhausted. When Beverly returned from speaking to the engineer he found a very distraught mistress. By the time the train got going again, I was looking forward to getting some much-needed sleep. But I couldn't help but ponder over the seemingly endless number of fascinating and intriguing characters I continued to meet on my journeys throughout the American West. Certainly it is one of the most fertile areas in the world for story material. In keeping with that, I recently read that the eminent Italian composer, Giacomo Puccini, was writing an opera called *The Girl of the Golden West*. It seems like a far cry from the more traditional operas, but on further thought I congratulate Maestro Puccini for venturing into an arena that I can vouch for as being fraught with interesting characters and stories.

I learned later that Belle Starr met her own fate near Jackson Rowe's house on a road from Fort Smith to her beloved Younger's Bend. Mixed reports had either her third husband Bill July, or a man named Edgar Watson killing her with two shotgun blasts. Each had a motive, although Mr. Watson seems to have the stronger. It seems Belle had turned a new leaf and announced that no outlaws could use Younger's Bend again as a hideout. Mr. Watson rented land to farm, but apparently was merely hiding from the law. When Belle Starr asked him to leave he argued, but then left — only to turn up right after Belle's murder. Mr. Watson had been at Jackson Rowe's house when Belle Starr stopped there for respite.

I marvel at how different life is in the American West for both men and women. It is a rugged existence, yet invigorating and exciting in its own unique way.

8

The Divine Sarah

"I am sure the Americans must be great lovers. They are so strong, so primitive, and so childish in their ardor. The English are wonderful men to love, because they possess the faculty of bending one to their likes, dislikes and moods without seeming to make it an imposition; but the Americans are greater, for they bend themselves to suit you." — *Sarah Bernhardt*

I have known Sarah Bernhardt since our first meeting in Brussels when she was visiting with Edward, the Prince of Wales. Sarah was a close friend of Princess Alexandra's, the two having spent many days together in the company of each other while the Prince traveled to and fro.

Sarah is, well, *Sarah.* There is no one else like her on this earth. She flaunts custom. She was the first woman to bid her dressmaker insert jewels in her slippers. She was the first woman to wear ostrich plumes as an ornament to her evening *coiffure.* She was the first woman audaciously to defy convention, and receive her friends in her painter's garb of silken pajamas! Whenever anyone starts a great outcry against her, others will shrug their shoulders and exclaim, *Mais, c'est Sarah!* She is Sarah. Answer enough. If ever a woman in France has been a law unto herself, it is Sarah Bernhardt — a whole lexicon of law, in fact. It was also Sarah who announced to the world, after meeting President Theodore Roosevelt in 1888, "Ah, but that man and I, we could rule the world!"

She is the most exciting and personable woman I have ever known. Which is why I was thrilled to greet her last week in St. Louis, and take her along with me in the Lalee to the Tabor Opera House in Denver, Colorado. She brought her entire repertoire and we performed two plays, the one which the French love so dearly, *Adrienne Lecouvreur* and the one with which she had so much to do with the writing, Alexander Dumas's *La Dame aux Camelias.*

It was *La Dame aux Camelias* — which Sarah often referred to simply as *La Dame* — that created so many ups and downs for poor Sarah — until finally in the end, she conquered both America on her first trip here — and then all of Europe, in spite of critics who seemed to scorn her so severely.

Critics only boosted Sarah's energy. She had a way of countering the critics and the cartoonists who viciously attacked her. When she found that the cartoonists had seized upon her slender figure and fuzzy hair as heaven-sent objects on which to exercise their talents, she wore clothes that accentuated her slimness, and her hair became more studiously unruly than ever. When she found that every foolish thing she did was immediately commented upon in a score of newspapers, hostile as well as friendly, she spent hours thinking out new escapades, and made foolishness an art.

The fact that Sarah could hold such men as Victor Hugo, Alexandre Dumas *fils,* Georges Clairin, Gustave Dore, and others like them, enthralled by the sheer power of her personality as partly expressed by her skill in conversation, is proof enough of her many-sided genius.

I use that word sparingly since she has upon occasion cautioned me, "Genius can be as eccentric as it pleases, but eccentricity without genius becomes a boomerang, to hurl fools into oblivion."

It is my opinion, based on what I know of Sarah, that she was the first actress among us who really understood the value of publicity, and the value of genius in the heart of talented people. I do hope her lessons have stuck to me and that I, too, have been able to apply intelligence to my career.

During our trip to Denver, Sarah told me the story of *La Dame*. She is such a wonderful story teller that I must record it for posterity here — in her words if I can possibly remember them all, although some of what I write down will most certainly be paraphrased:

"We were headed for my first trip to America. It was October of 1880. I had fallen into disfavor at the *Comedie Francaise* because of the critic Sarcey, when Alexandre Dumas *fils* brought *La Dame aux Camelias* to me for my earnest consultation. He had written it many years before and never had it performed.

"Let me take it with me!" I said and he gave the manuscript to me. A few days later I brought it back to him with a third of it crossed out and corrected. I had written new lines, adding to his manuscript at practically all the important passages and I had cut a great part of the second act out. Entirely!

"There!" I told him when I took his manuscript back. "Your play is better like that! If you will revise it as I have marked the manuscript, I will play it and make it a success."

Dumas was not pleased. "It is I," he declared angrily, "who am the playwright and not you, mademoiselle!"

I turned on my heel, headed for the door and barked back to him, "Very well! A day will come when you will beg me to produce your play!"

(Dumas refused to be influenced by such criticism, and eventually the play was produced, in a small way, at the *Comedie,* and then at another theater, but had no success at either. Sarah's amendments and suggestions had been ignored).

Sarah continued: After I organized my own company, Pierre Berton came to me with the information that Dumas wished to see me. "What about?" I asked.

"About a play called *La Dame aux Camelias.* We were reading it together last night and I believe it can be played by us with success. In fact, it is a play absolutely written for you!"

"Did you tell Dumas that?" I asked.

"Yes."

"What did he say?"

"He said that he agreed with me."

"And that was all?"

"That was all — except that he asked that I should bring the matter to your attention."

I laughed loudly and told Berton, "I told Dumas that he would one day beg me to play this thing for him, and you may tell him that if he wants me to, he must do just that — beg!"

The following day Berton brought Dumas to me. After meeting with him, where I demanded he beg, I accepted *La Dame aux Camelias.* It was accepted into our *repertoire.*

Sarah went on to explain that she first played *La Dame* at Brussels for King Leopold, who was still greatly enamored of Sarah. The play obtained no success whatever in Brussels. The Belgians preferred *Adrienne Lecouvreur* and *Froufrou. La Dame* it was that caused "Sarah's Epitaph," as written by Sarcey when she left the *Comedie.* In reference to her departure, he wrote that "it was time to send naughty children to bed." Sarah got the last laugh. When she returned from America — and her great success there — Sarcey was compelled to make a special journey to London in order to write reviews of Sarah's extraordinary productions there. But more about that later.

All the critics could not stop Sarah. Instead of sinking under the blow, Sarah only worked the harder. She was tireless at this period. It was during this time that Sarah met the Prince and Princess of Wales (while in Brussels).

But I digress. It is Sarah's experiences with Dumas and the play *La Dame* that I must continue to record here.

At the time, Sarah had fallen on hard times financially and learned that coming to America might provide her with enough money to continue on. Henry Irving discovered this and admonished Sarah.

"They tell me, Madame," he said to her, "that you are going to the United States?"

"Yes," said Sarah. "I must make money, and the Americans seem to have it all."

"Madame," Irving replied, "what you say saddens me. America is a country of barbarians! They know nothing about the theater, and yet they presume to dictate to us. If I were you I would not go to America! What you will gain in dollars, you will lose in heart-throbs at their ignorance of your art."

He was wrong. Sarah brought back from her first United States tour, six hundred thousand francs, and a profound respect for American free enterprise, and the reputation she had long been hoping to make for *La Dame aux Camelias*.

When Dumas discovered her intention to play *La Dame* in New York he cried disgustedly: "That's it! Try my play on the barbarians."

And therein lies the crux of Sarah's tale which I do my best to continue here:

"We opened in Booth's Theater in New York and it was filled on the first night with almost the entire French colony in New York," she said. "It seemed that the only Americans there were the critics along with a few wealthy society people who held their regular boxes. The first play we performed was *Adrienne Lecouvreur*."

The following day Abbey, the impresario, rushed into Sarah's bedroom waving a bundle of papers. He appeared grief stricken. He stopped abruptly, gave her an awful look — he could not speak.

"What is it?" she demanded. "The theater has been burned down, and my costumes are destroyed?"

"No, no," he said. "But your reputation is."

He showed her American newspapers that declared she was a magnificent actress, but that her *repertoire* was filled with plays that should not be shown on the American stage. The *Globe* said, "They are doubtless considered all right in immoral Paris, but they will certainly only succeed in disgusting Americans."

They tore *Adrienne Lecouvreur* to pieces. A play they called highly improper and one which should never be given in the presence of American women. Another paper demanded the police arrest Sarah and send her back to France. She was, needless to say, bewildered. "I had played all these in Paris, London, Brussels and in Copenhagen and had been met everywhere with tremendous applause.

"What I did not understand that first night, was that none of the American critics understood French, but possibly for a few words — and those words sent them off with wrong impressions."

"But," I interrupted her, "from end to end in English, the Americans would doubtless have found the plays insufferably vulgar."

"Lillie!" she retorted. "In French they are whimsical, delightful in their irony, and entirely free from anything objectionable whatsoever. It is simply that the American critics do not understand the subtlety of the lines. They have gathered their opinions solely from the action."

She continued: "The manager of the theater followed Abbey into my bedroom. He wore a strained, haunting look."

"You have seen the newspapers?" he asked.

"Yes." Consternation was in their eyes.

"What shall we do?" inquired Abbey.

"There is only one thing to do — we must choose another *repertoire!* They will have us arrested soon if this keeps up."

"But that is ridiculous," Sarah said angrily. "Never before in my life have I been so insulted! I will either play *La Dame aux Camelias* tonight, or I will pack up and return to France by the next boat."

Abbey cried out in protest.

"You can't do that," said Abbey. "There must be some way out of the difficulty."

"I shall play *La Dame aux Camelias* tonight, as arranged," I told them — clearly meaning these were my last words on the subject.

They argued with me for a while, but finally departed. Sarah learned later what they discussed. "She will leave,"

76

Abbey told the theater manager. "When Sarah Bernhardt makes up her mind, heaven and earth cannot change it."

"But we *must* do something," the manager said in despair.

"I have it!" exclaimed Abbey. "We will play *La Dame,* but we will call it something else. They will never know the difference."

So, when Sarah arrived at the theater that night she was astounded to see huge red placards outside, announcing that she would play *Camille.*

She immediately went to Jarret, the first man she met on the stage. "What is it, this *Camille?*" Sarah demanded furiously. "I know no *Camille.*"

"Oh yes, you do," Jarret answered, smiling. *"Camille* is — *La Dame!*"

I laughed uncontrollably when I heard that.

Sarah said, "And that night, the theater was packed, this time with a most representative crowd of Americans."

The publicity of the morning had done its work. Sarah Bernhardt was playing immoral pieces? Well, New York didn't know what to do about it, but New York decided to go and see for itself. Sarah invented the new benefits of a revue such as the ones she received her first night. Get the critics to call your play immoral, bribe the police to make a complaint about the immorality of one of the scenes — and then its success is assured!

New York loved *Camille* — enormously.

The critics were not fools, though. Every paper announced the next day that *Camille* was in reality *La Dame aux Camelias,* but with an American name.

Not unlike the critics and American press I have run into, the New York critics completely forgot their fulminations of only twenty-four hours before and said that it was an unthinkable crime that such a beautiful play should ever have been banned anywhere. It was rather *Frenchy,* they admitted, but Sarah's magnificent acting more than made up for that.

When Sarah returned to Europe after that run, Alexandre Dumas did not know whether to be delighted or dismayed. The "barbarians" had liked his play.

Also, upon her return, she found major success with *La Dame* in all of Europe. All of which may go to show that American audiences have a better sense of the dramatic than have audiences in Europe.

But it was her return to the *Comedie Francaise,* due to the success of her tour, that put Sarah back on top as the Queen of Paris forever.

After we performed in Denver to the loudest and most enthusiastic applause I have ever heard, the Divine Sarah bid goodbye for her final trip home.

Journalists continually try to imply that actresses such as myself, Sarah, and others are jealous of each other. This could not be further from the truth. On the contrary, we admire, respect and enjoy the fact that we are all sisters of the theater.

9

The Deadly Dentist

Nothing is more painful than an infected ear in cold weather, unless it's a toothache while waiting in the chair of a dentist whose reputation is somewhat suspect.

While Oscar visited the Matchless Mine in Leadville, I suffered a toothache (one of my molars) that caused me to seek out a dentist.

I remember at home on the Isle of Jersey, having a toothache when a child of ten. My mother took me to see a man she called "the doctor," but he wasn't. He practiced dentistry without a license, a matter I would know nothing about at the time. Unfortunately he also did not attend dental college in London or elsewhere. The pain he inflicted on me was dreadful enough to make me swoon.

Therefore, it was with great trepidation that I ventured to the dentist's office which was located in the back of Hyman's saloon on Harrison Street, not far from the Tabor Grand Hotel.

It was there that I met a winsome lady who called herself "Big Nose" Kate. Her nose was not as large as her sobriquet would suggest, but her outgoing nature was. She was the wife (I assumed at the time) of the dentist.

His name was Dr. John Holliday, and oh my, what a story she tells of him. Although I have met many Americans who seem already to be living legends, Dr. Holliday may top them all.

Dr. Holliday, I was pleased to learn, was a real dentist. He attended dental college in Baltimore, where, Kate explained, he came down with the consumption that makes him cough so much now. He was born in Griffin, Georgia, before the American Civil War, in March of 1852. His parents were Scottish, Henry B. and Alice Jane McKey Holliday. (There do seem to be many citizens here from Great Britain — a fact that does not make me uncomfortable).

Henry Holliday became wealthy as a farmer and landowner. They lived frugally (as most Scots do) and saved nearly everything they made — investing it in land. This seems to be a trait many of us from GB have, since even I have invested in much land here. I find this an interesting common instinct.

Dr. Holliday attended school at home, his teachers were his aunts, uncles and occasionally his mother. His father had served earlier as a volunteer in the war with Mexico. He had been one of Fannin's Avengers. Kate explained that Henry Holliday would tell stories to young John (the Doctor), about "sweeping the greasers out of Vera Cruz and up over the hills past the Cerro Gordo to Jalapa under a lone star banner reading across the top, "Young Hickory" and at the bottom, "Dallas and Victory." Kate laughed a sinister laugh when she told me this, adding that the old man never explained to his son about the miserable nights, the mud, the trenches, the Mexican cannon fire, the 6,000 men who did not return.

Dr. Holliday heard talk of war his entire life. When he was eight the vocabulary changed to "secession, states' rights, abolitionists and damned Yankees." The Yankees, he discovered, actually believed *Uncle Tom's Cabin* was a true story — therefore, you could not trust Yankees because you could not trust stupid people.

When John was nine, Georgia joined South Carolina (January 21, 1861). The American Civil War was underway and it proved devastating to the Holliday family just as it was to thousands of other Southern families.

But for Dr. Holliday in the early years, it was delightful. Soldiering after all was all glory — hadn't he heard that at home all his life?

What he did not understand in his youth was that wars were won with the deaths of thousands of young men, the destruction of property and through tactics not often understood even by the populace. "Like Scott's Anaconda," Kate told me. "Doc talks about it now sometimes, how a Yankee general named Winfield Scott blockaded the Southern states so tightly that they could not get supplies from anyone, at any time."

(I should interject here that Kate continually refers to the Doctor as "Doc" — an informality, I suppose, that is typically American, but one I have not yet been able to get used to.)

She then explained that Dr. Holliday's father was smart enough to move them to the Georgia coast (a place called Valdosta) where they were able to hold on to some land, even though another general named Sherman marched the Yankee army "to the sea," destroying everything in his path — including much of Henry Holliday's former property.

When the war was over, the family was destitute. Dr. Holliday had seen his strong, virulent father head off into battle for the Confederacy and come home sick, wounded and confused. Major Holliday, a man who had always had a short temper, returned with one that was shorter, (Kate called it a "hair trigger temper") violent. He was broke (except for his small land holdings), forty-two years old and unable to work.

Valdosta was also ruined by the Yankees. And when the railroad came through the area it missed Valdosta by four miles. So the citizens, in their effort to save their community, moved the town, each and every building, to the railroad, carrying every building, outhouse and lamppost the four miles to Valdosta's new location.

And built it up into a thriving community with the main street named after the man who drove the others to success: Holliday Street.

Henry Holliday also drove his son very hard. He was unrelenting in his goal to make sure his son had a profession that would always make him money. There were no schools in Valdosta when John was older so they formed a private school, which worked for a while.

On September 16, 1866, the Doctor's mother died. "The John Holliday everyone knew back then, also died," Kate said. "He won't tell you that, but he has told me. She was everything to him. His father was nothing. He hated his father because he pushed him so hard, drove him with anger and a temper that flared so quickly no one ever knew when it was coming."

John's father remarried a year later. "He took a twenty-four year old named Rachel, a woman in black," Kate explained. "A war widow." He married because he needed someone to care for his house.

I suggested that maybe his father was trying to hold on to respectability by having a wife. Kate smiled, nodded and said, "Yes, but Doc won't admit that. He doesn't believe in that stuff, unless he's facing down another man with a gun. Then he demands respect, but not the kind his father wanted."

John did respect his father for one thing. Major Holliday knew he could regain his wealth if he became a Yankee sympathizer, but he refused. He would not be a Scallawag. John's father, for all his other faults, became the Valdosta mayor, a member of Masons and charter-signer of both. He was a hard worker for the improvement of his town and the county of Lowndes.

John's bitterness toward the remarriage was held within him, an anger he harbored for many years. Since they were Scottish, clannish matters would be kept within the family. Relatives were always about, but no one ever discussed the family faults.

"Then he met her," Kate said softly, turning her attention away from me, looking out the window upon Harrison Street.

"Who?"

"Mattie Holliday. His first cousin. A Catholic girl. He's been in love with her all his life."

I did not challenge her statement, nor did I press to understand better her relationship with Dr. Holliday. I have come to learn that we each, in our own way, make do with the love we give and with the love we take.

"He used to be a happy, gay fellow," Kate explained. "But he told me he also had his father's temper, even when he was a teenager. Mattie calmed him," she added quietly. "That's something I've not been able to do. Instead, we've fought a lot. Really bad sometimes. I've even tried to kill him. Shot six bullets at him in a hotel room in Dodge City, but he's too quick and I'm not very good with a pistol."

I was stunned. "How are things now?" I asked, I believe more interested in her response for purposes of analyzing my own chances in his dental chair than in her chances as a paramour.

She smiled. "He's sick with consumption. He drinks too much to kill the pain. Otherwise, he's settled down a lot."

"Oh, my," I said, hoping I didn't appear too apprehensive.

"He went to dental college in Baltimore," she reassured me. "He was eighteen years old when he left. That's where he got the consumption. That's also where he learned to play Faro and where he learned about gambling. He worked for a while as a dentist in Griffin, Georgia, with an older dentist. The consumption bothered him so much though, that he moved to Atlanta hoping that would help. Atlanta was still burned out from the war, but it was rebuilding quickly. Doc got into trouble in Atlanta, gambling at Faro tables that were illegal.

"Atlanta's where he learned about his consumption. He saw a doctor there after he spit up some blood.

"The doctor told him back then, I think it was about fifteen years ago, that he would have six months to live if he stayed in Georgia, a year or two at the most if he moved to the high country in Texas. The doctor told him he would die a strangling death in his sleep."

Kate said plainly after that, "That was the end of young Dr. John Holliday, the dentist. He became 'Doc' Holliday, the gambler and killer after that."

Dr. Holliday moved to Dallas, Texas. He continually wrote to Mattie, explaining what he had learned, telling her he could not possibly marry her until he was better and until he had something to offer her. Some time during all this correspondence, Mattie wrote back that she would enter a convent and become a nun. When she did, he was devastated.

In Dallas he took up dentistry and gambling for a living — an odd combination to be sure, but he was not a man to roll with the tide.

The Julian Bogel's "swell" saloon became his home away from home. He took up drinking with a serious effort to kill the pain of consumption.

It was 1873, and the Eastern states were plunged into the worst depression in the nation's history. The people began a mass migration toward the West, in search of work, land, a way to make a living. The East's problems became the West's growth.

"Doc tried every cure from snake oils to whisky," Kate told me. "In the end, the whisky won him over. But that didn't happen in a day. For a long while, he was a very respected businessman in Dallas."

"I have played Faro," I told her. "It's a complicated game, one that requires a man's full attention and concentration."

"That's why Doc likes it. It takes his mind off his pain. He is so good at the game that no one ever beats him." She smiled again and told me, "By the way, the professional gambler deals Faro and plays poker."

By the time he was recognized in Dallas as a gambling man and a heavy drinker, his personality began to change to that of an untrustworthy, untruthful and unpredictable man who cared for no one but himself. When he was sober he was irritable and often exploded into violent rages. He had become a sick man, mentally and physically and hanging out in honky-tonks contented him.

85

Finally, the medical doctor's estimated two years of life were up. And he was still alive — but living on borrowed time.

"You might call it a tragic comedy," Kate said, "like some of your plays. He became the fair-haired youth pursued by a cruel fate — only he didn't die. Each new day kept showing up. Finally, he couldn't take it anymore."

She pulled out an old, faded and folded newspaper article from the *Dallas Herald* of January 2, 1875. She read, "Dr. Holliday and Mr. Austin, a saloon-keeper, relieved the monotony of the noise of fire-crackers by taking a couple of shots at each other yesterday afternoon. The cheerful note of the peaceful six-shooter is heard once more among us. Both shooters were arrested."

"Doc" (I find myself using Kate's abbreviation for "Doctor" less reluctantly than before after hearing her repeat it so often and with such ease) Holliday was requested by the local authorities to leave town, which he did, only to end up two weeks later in a little log jail in Fort Griffin, Texas. This was truly the beginning of the legend of a man who was about to work on my aching tooth.

He gave up dentistry, deciding that gambling was a surer thing. These were his people now, the saloonkeepers, bunco people, the prostitutes and gamblers. No pretenses, no cushion seats, no frills. He was an alcoholic now, a gunslinger and a devoted professional gambler. (This did not build my confidence for him to work on my tooth.)

"Politicians came to town," Kate said. "That meant the usual 'clean out of the prostitutes and gamblers.' Righteous stuff," she said. "Hell, Doc didn't even shoot anybody and they threw him in jail 'cause he'd been in jail in Dallas for a shooting. So, him being smart and all, he puts up bail and hops the next stage out of town."

Straight to Denver, Colorado, where he arrived as Tom McKey — a name he chose in order to hide the reputation that preceded him.

He went right to work as a Faro dealer for Charley Foster at Babbitt's House on Blake Street. He continued to drink heavily, but because he drank so much and was rarely sober, his personality remained for the most part, calm. His pay amounted to about seven dollars a day. Meals cost him "two-bits" (American slang for a quarter of a dollar) and a hotel room cost a dollar a day. "The job was worth keeping," Kate told me, "especially since he had no other way to make a living."

Kate also told me that Doc spent hours upon hours practicing with cards, finally learning a very flashy way to shuffle, cut and break up a deck. He learned even more important card handling by developing undetectable false cuts, dealing seconds off the bottom and to stack a deck right in front of everyone — once again — undetected.

Denver was growing then. Its population was 18,000 and none of those toted guns except for police and streetcar conductors who had to protect their passengers and themselves from some smalltime Jesse James characters. Denver was a combination of law-abiding citizens and a few who were not law-abiding.

For two years Doc made a living off both of them. Then came the gold-rush of the Dakotas. "Everyone was headed to Cheyenne, Wyoming Territory," Kate explained. "From there, they could easily get to the Black Hills gold.

Kate pulled out another newspaper clipping. It was from the *Wyoming Weekly Leader*, dated February 12, 1876. It said, "A fresh invoice of Denver gamblers and sneaks arrived yesterday. That dying town seems to be 'taking a puke' as it were, of this class of citizen."

Doc stopped in Cheyenne for a while, where he dealt Faro while living in ease at Ford's place. "He kept an eye on the news about the Black Hills gold because the Indians were hoppin' mad and a General named Custer was supposed to go clean them out. Only he failed." Everyone headed for a place called Deadwood Gulch after that.

"Deadwood City," Kate said, "became the place to work." So, Doc headed there and met up with Wild Bill Hickok and Calamity Jane. Doc was there when a man called Jack McCall walked into a saloon and shot Wild Bill in the back.

"Ever since then, Doc has sat with his back to the wall. You see, Wild Bill always sat with his back to the wall just so's he wouldn't be shot. When Doc played Faro with him, Doc had to sit opposite him and was always exposed. Hickok would tell him, 'Best you remember this, Doc. They's a lot of gunslingers out there lookin' for a reputation.'

"So, when they were playing the night he got shot, Doc had told him, 'Okay Bill, tonight I sit with my back to the wall.' Hickok let him. Doc said he laughed, ordered drinks around and then they started playing. This McCall came in through a back door, slipped up behind Hickok and shot him dead."

She told me there were a lot of killings in Deadwood after that. Each one was reported in the papers and Kate had a stack of them. She also informed me that it was in Deadwood where Doc Holliday met Wyatt Earp. Wyatt was a young man looking for some fame. His first official posse was when he rode out with others to look for the killer of the local marshal's son, Johnny Slaughter.

"When winter came up, the gamblers always took off for Cheyenne and Doc was with them, except he kept on going to Denver that year," Kate said. "Winters in Cheyenne weren't much better than winters in Deadwood. And in

Denver more people passed through town. Traveling gamblers always talked to the local gamblers about the other parts of the territory and where the money was."

Which is how Doc Holliday learned about Dodge City, Kansas, and the money that passed through town from the cattle drives.

The year was 1878. It was the worst year of the depression. Over 14,000 businesses failed that year. More people poured into Denver — bringing with them mostly trouble. Denver began to drag its tail. So, when spring came and the financial outlook failed to improve in Denver, "Tom McKey" headed off to Dodge City.

"And damned if Dodge City ain't where I met him," Kate beamed. "He was a skinny, sickly little runt with a big mouth, a big gun and a mean temper. But I fell hard for him anyway — even though I don't think he ever fell that hard for me. It was always Mattie this and Mattie that. A phantom woman I never met. A nun, of all things, taking first place over me!"

During his time in Denver and Deadwood City, Doc had figured out how to "get around the law," and no longer feared using his real name. When he left Denver, he left Tom McKey behind, and once again traveled as J. H. Holliday.

He had become the *beau ideal* of professional gamblers. He was quiet, gentlemanly appearing and as fast with his hands and mind as greased lightning. "Neither could they mess with his mind with liquor, smooth talking phonies, or women" Kate said with a glow. "Until he met me, of course!"

Kansas is so flat, as they say, you can stand on one end of the state and see the other. In the middle of this was Dodge City, situated at a long-used ford across the Arkansas River, five miles west of Fort Dodge on the old Santa Fe trail. It was originally built by H.L. Sitler, a teamster who supplied wood at the fort and built the camp for buffalo hunters and freighters. It was called Buffalo City for a long while.

I remember a stage trip from Kansas City to Dodge City when I played the Comique in Dodge. (It used to be called The Lady Gay or Springer's Opera House, but the name was changed the year I visited). The stage coach ride was bump, bump, bump and dust, dust, dust all the way. And it was very, very hot.

(The other billing at the Comique during that visit was an American named Eddie Foy — and I remember he was almost shot. His suit was hanging in the dressing room when a large gunfight took place outside. Three bullets passed through the building and through his suit).

Doc checked into the Dodge House, the city's main hotel. "On his first day in town he met Luke Short, another man who gambled a lot, but was also a gunfighter. Luke invited Doc into a game and that was it. He never stopped ruling Dodge City with the cards until he left."

Kate told me they used to call the men who herded the cows "herders," but while Luke and Doc were there, they started calling them "cow-boys." (The word was hypenated at first, she said.)

Dodge was in the path of the big trail drives of cattle that came up from Texas. They used to take a route to Abilene called the Chisholm Trail but the Texas cattle started to catch tick fever along that trail and the herders shifted to the new trail.

The cow-boys weren't gunslingers or Rover boys, but neither were they innocent. They came in all colors, dispositions and sizes — mostly they stopped off at Dodge to have a good time.

And Doc Holliday and his peers were prepared to oblige.

But like many of the remote towns in the West, Dodge became a breeder of six-shooter evil. One of Doc's new friends and allies, Marshal Ed Masterson was killed while on duty by two cowboys, Jack Wagner and Alf Walker. They were under the influence of whisky and had already had one run-in with Mr. Masterson. Ed Masterson was twenty-six years old.

After this shooting, Doc once again met Wyatt Earp. Earp had come to town seeking Ed Masterson's job, but he had already been replaced by Charles E. Bassett. Bassett quickly appointed Wyatt Earp an assistant marshal.

Wyatt and Doc became friends. "Well, anyway, they got along with each other," Kate clarified.

Dodge was full of "ladies of the evening." One of these, one who appeared the youngest was a tall, big-nosed, bosomy brunette.

"Me," Kate laughed. "It was my nose that attracted Doc to me."

"And why did you find him attractive?" I asked.

"Like I said before, he was classy, with pain hidden in his eyes. I screamed with delight."

And it would seem that at first Doc tried to rid himself of Kate, but she wouldn't permit it. She drove him crazy. Everywhere Doc went, Kate was there. "Wyatt told Doc to spank me, to slug me on the chin if he had to. That's how to handle these floozies," he said. She laughed. "But all Doc could do was cough. 'Sides, if he took a poke at me, I'd knock him colder'n Kansas in January."

"Sounds like a match made in heaven," I said without much meaning attached to it.

"Aha! Of course. Doc says it works 'cause I don't have any brains to bother him with — never give out no heavy problems. I have a healthy body," at which she stood and raising her light dress whirled around for me to see. I must say, it certainly did appear to be healthy. She continued, "And I know every cuss word in the English language and just like Doc, I like whisky. So, what do you think? Is this a good team or not?"

I did not respond other than to smile. But I did say to myself only that possibly Doc loved her roughness more than her beauty, loved her vulgarity more than the love that came from her — because if he was in love with Mattie, as Kate declared, then to choose one such as Kate left him with little guilt or shame.

"One night," Kate told me, "Doc went to bed early upstairs in Deacon Cox's hostelry and it miffed me bad. So I got my six-shooter and went up to his room and banged down his door. I figured he was just trying to get away from me. So I yelled at him that he was a no-good son of a bitch for treating me that way and I began shooting at him. He was quick. He could dance a jig like nobody when you shot at him. I put two bullets into the bed and missed him and four more into the air, but all that happened was that he tackled me and we fell into the bed and that was the best love making I ever had."

Apparently for the next ten days they weren't seen by anybody in town. Doc and Kate never separated again.

"Why have you come to Leadville to reside?" I asked.

Kate turned away from me for a moment, then said, "Doc came here to die. I truly believe that. He is so sick that I think he has provoked fights just to get someone to shoot him dead."

"That's awful," I replied, shocked at the suggestion.

"You see," Kate said, leaning toward me so she could lower her voice, "Doc is sick with pneumonia, and still gets dizzy from the altitude here. Cy Allen fired him last week for getting into a fight with one of Johnny Tyler's crowd and that's made Doc even sicker. He's unemployed and broke right now."

I admit to being confused by this exposition. I had gone there for Dr. Holliday to look at my aching tooth and thought he was fully employed doing the same for others.

"No," Kate said. "Doc comes in, passes out on the cot in his office and waits. But no patients come. Everyone in town knows who he is, and they joke behind his back that the only way he knows how to fix a tooth is to shoot it out."

I sat back hard into my chair. No way was I going to let "Doc" Holliday fix my tooth.

Kate kept on talking. "Johnny Tyler formed this gang of Doc-haters to help get rid of Doc. He wants Doc dead, but won't openly threaten to kill him. It's all 'cause of what Doc did to him in Tombstone."

"Which was?"

"They had a showdown in Tombstone. Tyler backed down, in front of the whole town and never could come back. He still won't draw down on Doc, 'cause he's just plain scared of him. I mean even with Doc so sick, hardly able to pull his gun from his pouch, Tyler won't face him. So instead, he's just gone around town forming this group of people who say bad things about Doc and help get him fired."

"Can't you do something? Maybe get this Allen fellow to hire him back?"

"It's the other Allen, Billy Allen, no relationship to Cyrus, who I'm afraid of. He's a bartender at the Monarch saloon and one of Tyler's closest allies. He loaned Doc five dollars last week and now he demands its return. Doc was thinking he could get it from you for looking at your tooth. Billy Allen said he'd lick the stuffing out of Doc if he didn't fork over the five. I think it was all a set up, arranged by Tyler."

Just then, the door to Doc's back room where he must have been sleeping off his pain opened and he slowly staggered out, heading straight for the cigar case near the bar. I watched curiously, in complete wonderment because he was such a small, slight man — with such a huge legend which included a major gunfight in Dodge City that everyone knew about. His hands shook slightly when he reached for a cigar but they steadied suddenly when a man burst through the entrance to the saloon. It was Billy Allen. Kate stood up and headed for Doc, but Doc held his hand up for her to stop. She did, with a gasp, bringing her own right hand to her mouth. She glanced to me and I think that I have never seen such fear in a person's eyes before.

Allen shouted to Doc, "I've come for my money, Doc."

But Doc already had his cut off Colt .44 up and he fired a shot which missed Allen and went through the glass of the folding door. Allen turned to run away, but stumbled and fell. Doc reached across the cigar case and fired a second shot. He hit Allen in the right arm from the rear between the shoulder and elbow.

A Mr. Kellerman got hold of Doc at that point and stopped him from firing a third shot. Allen got up and left but fainted outside. He was placed into a hack and driven to his room where Doctors Maclean and D'Avignon dressed his wound.

After the second shot was fired Captain Bradbury rushed in and disarmed Doc, then arrested him. Kate was beside herself, somewhat in shock. I went to her, but as I did so,

I heard Doc telling Captain Bradbury, "Protect me. Don't let anyone shoot me in the back."

I should say that Bill Hickok's death had a firm impact on Doc Holliday.

I never again saw Katie Elder after that event. I was able to take care of my toothache with the help of a dentist whose name was Dr. Thomas Kelly, a longtime resident of Leadville.

And needless to say, I was happy to leave Leadville behind, although I enjoyed playing the Tabor Opera House very much.

Late note: Doc was brought to trial a few months later, but all that happened to him was that he was asked to leave town — which he did right away. He ended up in Glenwood Springs at the local sanatorium where he died on November 8, 1887 at the age of 35. The only possession they found on him was a box of letters — correspondence from a Sister of Charity, in Atlanta, Georgia. They were from his cousin, Mattie.

And so ended my first-hand meeting with Kate Elder and Doc Holliday. But, it was not the last I would hear of the unfortunate dentist.

10

Mark of the Savage

The days of the West were both exciting and dangerous, none more so than for the brave pioneers who risked their lives in making the long and arduous trek across the country during the early part of this century.

While riding in the luxurious comfort of the Lalee and gazing at the panoramic vistas of desert passing before me outside my window, I oftentimes thought of those gallant pioneers who crossed the broad width of America in conditions that would have discouraged the great majority of people. I wondered if I would have had the grit to move across America in a covered wagon or some other primitive mode of transportation? After all, these travelers had made their way West not that many years ago, but it was a time when there was no transcontinental railway and even worse, few known roads on which they could guide their way. They were the pathfinders, men, women and children of such rugged constitutions that they should forever be remembered by the generations of Americans who will come after them and settle the cities to the West that their sacrifices made possible.

Even to this day, as the years and months of this century gradually but surely wend their way toward the next hundred years, there are still sections of Western America that have uprisings by the natives that are proving troublesome to the settlers and ranchers who are trying to make a new life in this giant nation. But, thankfully, there seems to be an era of peace dawning for the future and I hope it will be to all parties' satisfaction, settlers and natives alike. For while I am a firm believer in the progress of civilization, it cannot be forgotten that the Indians, whose home this was before the coming of the white man, have a right to live and exist in harmony on a land that was once entirely their own.

The scars of the continuing unrest between white man and Indian are still evident, even to this day. This was brought home to me in stark reality on my most recent tour of the Western portion of America, when our troupe was playing in the village of Santa Barbara, California.

It was there that I met and heard, first-hand, the story of one of America's most famous female Indian captives, Olive Oatman.

Olive was a woman in her mid forties when I met her. She was very attractive and in her youth undoubtedly would have been called quite beautiful. Except for one thing. The poor woman had some unsightly black marks running from just beneath her lower lip down the entire length of her jaw. At first look one thought they were birthmarks, but their color was not the usual purplish-pink, but coal black. Naturally, it would not be ladylike to inquire as to the nature of the blemishes, but when Olive approached me and asked for my autograph, I'm sure she observed me looking at the marks as much as I tried to avoid making it obvious.

Thankfully, my *faux pas* did not seem to upset her.

"May I explain these markings on my chin, Mrs. Langtry?" she asked.

I was caught completely unprepared. Then, after the sudden flush that had reddened my cheeks subsided somewhat, I was finally able to respond.

"Oh, my dear," I said, "I apologize for being so obvious in my look. It is really none of my — or anyone's — business."

"No need to apologize, ma'am," she said, "it is something that I was not able to discuss for many years, but now that I can freely talk about it, it is much less painful for me."

I nodded reassuringly, still trying as best I could to put the *gaffe* behind me. "You are a lovely woman," I told her, "and whatever pain you have suffered you have handled well."

"Most likely because of the passing of years," she told me. "Time does, as has been said, heal all wounds."

Olive Oatman then related to me one of the most astounding stories I have ever heard in my lifetime.

It had its beginnings in 1851, when Olive was just in her early teens. She and her family were bound for California in a wagon train, her father, like so many thousands before and after him, hoping to find his fortune in the newly discovered gold mines in the West.

As I have said, the trips were fraught with danger. Not only were the roads barely passable, the weather could be treacherous, unfriendly Indians were always a threat, and there was the fear of the unknown lurking every inch of the way. In addition, the majority of the wagon parties were inexperienced travelers, relying almost exclusively on their wagon masters and scouts to lead them safely across the country.

While making their way across the vast desert, Olive's father, eager and anxious to make up as much ground on the long and arduous journey as possible, suddenly found his wagon a great distance ahead of the rest of the train.

"We had lost sight of the main wagon train, which had stopped to assist some members whose wagon had lost its wheel," Olive remembered. "My father refused to stop and we pressed on, but suddenly we were far ahead of the others and apparently made a wrong turn into a large and desolate valley and were irretrievably lost."

There was no need to panic, Olive's father told everyone, but the look in his eye could not conceal the worry that had come over him. As he tried to retrace his wagon back in the direction they had come, suddenly the terrifying screams of Indians shattered the calm. Their war clubs swinging menacingly in the air, the Yavapai warriors were quickly upon the group. Olive's father was the first one felled, killed instantly, before he could even get to his rifle. Then her mother felt the deadly blow of a Yavapai club. Olive's teenage brother, Lorenzo, trying to loosen his father's rifle from underneath his prone body, was struck so hard he was knocked from the side of the wagon and crumbled beneath it in a heap.

Only Olive and her seven year old sister Mary Ann were left. They were holding onto each other in fright, the poor girls having seen their family slaughtered before their very eyes. Now they awaited the blows that would mean their deaths. But the blows never came. They did not know that it was the custom of many Indian tribes to carry off their female victims, especially the young ones, and eventually use them as wives or, more frighteningly, sell them as slave laborers.

Olive and Mary Ann spent a year as slaves of the Yavapais, then were walked North to the Colorado River settlement of another tribe, the Mohaves, where they were sold, once again as slave laborers.

Life under the Mohaves became slightly more tolerable for the girls. Beatings were not as frequent as they had been while they were the captors of the Yavapais and the girls were permitted to grow their own food, mainly corn and melons.

In 1853, two years after Olive and her family had begun their trip West, a drought struck the area of the Mohaves and the majority of the tribe starved to death, including Mary Ann, who was frail and still traumatized from the terrible event that had overcome her and her family.

"I was now alone," Olive said. "I realized no one knew what had become of me and I had given up all hope of ever being freed from my bondage with the Mohaves. My feelings could not have sunk to any lower depths."

But here the story took a turn that one would only expect to find only in a work of fiction. Olive was *not* alone. Her brother, Lorenzo, left for dead after the Yavapai attack, had, in fact, survived the massacre. He was obsessed with the desire to find and free his sisters. Unstintingly, he searched for five long years with no success, not having an inkling as to where they might be or, in fact, that they were even still alive. Lorenzo would not give up. Eventually, his determination paid off. He located a Yuma Indian who admitted he knew of Olive's whereabouts. Finally, through some skilful bargaining, Lorenzo was able to purchase Olive's freedom.

The first sight of Olive was shocking. Dressed in Indian garments, her face tanned the color of leather, her black hair braided in the manner of Indian squaws, she was hardly recognizable. Worst of all, in the tradition of Mohave women, Olive had been tattooed on the arms, chin and jawline. The method, she told me, was to pierce the skin and force charcoal or black dye into the wounds, thus the black color of the markings.

Olive was in a daze when she was released. She had not seen nor spoken to a white person in over five years. In fact, she barely remembered how to speak English, not having said a word in her own language for all that time.

The physical suffering that Olive had undergone was apparent. But even more damaging was the mental abuse. She was forever set apart with the garish tattoos the Indians had applied to her face and body. The memories of her life with the Indians were so vivid that when first rescued she could not speak. She would only sit, mute, with her disfigured face buried in her hands. A friend recalled that Olive had always been "quiet and reserved," but now "the great suffering of her early life set her apart from the rest of the world."

Some cynics claimed that if they had been in Olive's situation they would have preferred to have killed themselves rather than undergo the life of an Indian captive. Olive could only answer by agreeing with another former Indian captive, Fanny Wiggins Kelly, who wrote of her experiences, "It is only those who have looked over the dark abyss of death who know how the soul shrinks from meeting the unknown future. While hope offers the faintest token of refuge, we pause upon the fearful brink of eternity, and look back for rescue."

Captives such as Olive and Fanny exhibited a tremendous amount of bravery and fortitude to endure the life of a captive and slave and live to tell about it. And to think most of the women like Olive were innocent young girls when they were captured makes their stories even more awe inspiring.

The Olive Oatman story, I am happy to report, had a happy ending. This gallant woman, who suffered a fate as a young girl beyond the imagination of most of us, eventually recovered and has taken her rightful role in society. She regained her speech well enough to go on a lecture tour and relate her frightening experiences to enthralled audiences. In fact, when I met her, she was on her way to Northern California to give a series of lectures. And, the man who was with her, I was pleased to learn, was her husband.

Olive told me that even though she realized she would be branded with the mark of the Mohaves for the rest of her life and that she would be subjected to inquisitive stares as long as she lived, she was no longer intimidated by the looks but, actually, wore the marks as a badge of honor.

"You are a remarkable woman, Olive Oatman," I told her.

She just looked at me with a smile and thanked me.

They say that women are actually the stronger of the species. I dare not enter into that discussion. But there is no question in my mind that brave women like Olive Oatman are a tribute to the entire human race.

11

Little Girl, Big Talent

I often think about how life presents so many surprising twists and turns. But are they really as unplanned as we believe?

There are some who say that whatever happens to us in this life is predestined. Their theory is that from the moment we are born, the entire panorama of events of our lifetime has been planned in advance by, I suppose, the almighty Himself or, at least, by one of His very close associates. So, based upon that line of thinking, all our fortunes and misfortunes leave us little or no control over what eventually happens to us during the course of our individual lifetimes.

It is an interesting supposition, but not one to which I subscribe. Admittedly, at times it is a theory that is tempting to believe in — after all, what better excuse for a wrong deed than to say "it was predestined and I had no control over it?" Be that as it may, I favor the hypothesis that we are put on this earth to make our own way, that nothing is predestined but that the unexpected and unplanned can influence our lives in ways we could never have imagined — or planned. And that is what makes life interesting, is it not? The unexpected can be exciting, invigorating and challenging.

All of which leads me to a story of one of America's most popular performers whose career, I strongly believe, was inspired by a most unexpected relationship during her youth.

I first met Lotta Crabtree when we were both in New York. She was, at the time, nearing the end of a long and illustrious career on the stage which had its beginnings in the gold mining area of California. I am quite familiar with that part of the Golden State, having played many theaters in the region myself. In fact, as I have duly reported elsewhere in this journal, I am a California landowner, the proud mistress of Langtry Ranch near the same region where Lotta first gained fame and fortune. But we never crossed paths in California since she was performing there some years before my career took me to the U.S.

Lotta was born in New York in 1847 and was of English descent. Her mother, who was to play an enormous part in her life, was Mary Ann Livesley and her father was John Ashworth Crabtree. As happened to so many families during the middle part of the century, the Crabtrees soon found themselves in the mining country of California, attracted by the dreams of a quick and easy fortune which never came to pass — at least not from the discovery of gold by Mr. Crabtree.

John Crabtree was determined to "strike it rich," as the saying goes, and spent much of his time away from his family, prospecting the fields for that elusive precious metal that, he hoped, would make him an instant millionaire. Meanwhile, Mary Ann and infant daughter Lotta were left to fend for themselves as best they could in the booming California mining town of Grass Valley, where, I have been told, one mine alone produced more than four-million dollars in gold. It is no wonder then, at that time, Grass Valley, with a population of three thousand, was one of the fastest-growing cities in California, larger than Oakland, Los Angeles and San Diego. Despite the rough-and-tumble atmosphere one often found in these mining towns, there was a code of honor amongst the men whereby a virtuous woman was treated almost with veneration. In fact, in describing this attitude one journalist wrote:

"Every miner seemed to consider himself her sworn guardian, policeman and protector, and the slightest dishonorable word, action or look of any miner or other person would have been met with a rebuke he would remember so long as he lived. If, perchance, he survived the chastisement."

Thus, despite the absence of her husband for great periods of time, Mrs. Crabtree had no concern for her or her daughter's safety and supported herself and Lotta by running a boardinghouse in the town. It was while the Crabtrees were living here that fate stepped in and forever changed the life of the little girl.

Imagine, if you will, how unlikely it would be that a beautiful, exotic woman, known throughout the great salons of Europe as the mistress of the king of Bavaria, the intimate friend of such luminaries as Alexander Dumas, Victor Hugo and George Sand, would be transposed several thousand miles to a mining town in the heart of California's gold rush country, and you have invoked the real-life image of none other than the notorious Lola Montez.

I take the liberty of calling Miss Montez "notorious" not in any derogatory sense of the word but more in awe of the notoriety she gained during her career as one of the preeminent stage performers of the early part of this century.

I will not dwell on the intriguing life story of Lola Montez here because I have already written about it at some length in another entry in this journal. Suffice it to say that I will discuss Miss Montez in this chapter only as she pertains to Lotta Crabtree.

As I hope I have made clear, it has always amazed me that Lotta Crabtree, an elfin six-year-old living in Grass Valley, California, would have her life influenced by so unlikely a personage as Lola Montez. But it happened and it is a well-documented fact.

Lola, as it turns out, had been touring the United States, playing cities and hamlets that criss-crossed the vast nation much the same as my troupe has been doing on this and previous trips. Her tour took her to the mining communities of California and she and her new American husband eventually bought a home in Grass Valley, where Lola, now in the sunset of her career, hoped to settle down in quiet retirement. But this lively woman was not cut out for such a lifestyle, not after her tumultuous career both on and off the stage. (I can sympathize with her. Retirement is a synonym for boredom in my vocabulary and I hope to pursue my acting career as long as audiences will have me.)

Lola ran her Grass Valley home much as she would if it had been in Paris or London. Interestingly, there were many Europeans in Grass Valley, the majority of whom were French, thus allowing Lola to entertain in the grand manor to which she had been accustomed on the continent.

But living only two doors away from the Montez home was petite Lotta Crabtree who, at her tender age, was no doubt mightily intrigued by this famous actress-neighbor and the chatter of gossiping matrons of the town about the world-famous entertainer.

Lola soon got to know Lotta and took a motherly interest in the pretty child with her strawberry curls and vibrant personality. Lola taught Lotta some dances and some of the ballads she had used in her own act. Then she took the little girl horseback riding and soon thereafter Lotta became an expert rider. They say that most actors and actresses are bitten by a mysterious little "bug" that forever binds them to life on the stage no matter how successful — or unsuccessful — they are. I must confess my entrance into the acting world was more predicated on the necessity to earn a living than anything else, but I have had the pleasure to meet innumerable performers who have dedicated their lives to the stage. Whatever her motivation, little Lotta Crabtree, soon after meeting and becoming more or less the protege of Lola Montez, was performing for the local citizenry and had been launched on a career on the stage that would endure for many years thereafter.

Lotta's first performance, as the story goes, was dancing an Irish jig for a group of appreciative miners in the village of Rough and Ready (such a colorful name!) which was just West of Grass Valley. Was her mentor, Lola Montez, in attendance, proudly observing little Lotta's unpretentious debut? Probably not, but I like to think Lotta gave her performance with Lola's encouragement and blessing.

The performance in Rough and Ready, as it turns out, was actually a prelude to Lotta's official debut, which came about a year later after her father had moved the Crabtree family to the town of Rabbit Creek. It seems that a local theater owner, vainly searching for a child actress to compete with a rival whose small daughter was gaining in popularity with local audiences, spotted Lotta and came up with the idea of putting her to work on his stage.

A great many of the miners were Irish, so when Lotta appeared on stage in a delightful green costume her mother had made for her, embellished by a pair of Irish brogues and the ever-present shillelagh made by her father, she was an instant hit. Her performance was regarded as nothing short of sensational by the appreciative Irishmen, who backed up their enthusiasm by deluging the stage with sacks of gold dust and nuggets worth up to fifty dollars.

Thus began Lotta's long and successful career, now masterminded by her ever-present mother, Mary Ann. There was no need at this time to travel too far out of the immediate area of the multitude of mining camps in the vicinity, because the audiences there were starved for entertainment and the talented Lotta was fast becoming the reigning favorite of the hard-working gold miners.

But it was a grueling life, made up mostly of one-night stands which saw Lotta and Mary Ann arrive in a town during the day, give a performance, and soon be on their way to the next town some miles away. And the two ladies did this on their own, because Lotta's father was determined to continue his search for gold, still not realizing that his real "gold" was in the form of his multi-talented young daughter.

Lotta soon began to increase her repertoire, learning new songs and dances. A Negro minstrel taught her to do the soft-shoe and from others she picked up the buck-and-wing. In addition she was becoming an expert at pantomime, and soon she had expanded her vistas from the mining camps to the largest city in California, San Francisco.

Despite some antics that would be considered outrageous if presented by other performers, Lotta had a knack of endearing herself to her audiences and soon winning them over to her side. When she plopped a large cigar in her mouth and began smoking it — a "bit" she undoubtedly learned from Lola Montez, who had used it herself on the stage some years prior — she was greeted by thunderous laughter rather than shock by her audiences, which included local matrons who would have been indignant at the unladylike gesture had it been anyone other than loveable Lotta.

Lotta was a master of humor and pathos, oftentimes bringing her audiences to tears before quickly turning her drama to comedy to completely reversing her admiring fans' emotions. She could run the gamut from skillful acting to downright buffoonery and was a master of improvisation. She would titillate her audiences by swirling her skirts to reveal several layers of underslips or even a bare ankle. But it was all done in innocent good fun under the watchful eye of Mary Ann, and Lotta's popularity increased to the point where by the time she had reached her teens it was deemed she should advance her career by appearing in New York.

As I can well attest, New York critics are oftentimes not as appreciative as those on the West Coast. Lotta's debut in New York was less than successful, and her confidence was somewhat shaken as she set out on what became a three-year tour that took her to the major cities of the East Coast and the Midwestern sections of the U.S.

But the indomitable Lotta soon was back in good form and her persistence won over not only the audiences, but the Eastern critics as well. She was well on her way to becoming the favorite comedienne in the nation when she returned to New York to appear in the leading role in *Little Nell and the Marchioness*. The play, adapted from Dickens'

The Old Curiosity Shop, was an instant hit and Lotta now had reached the pinnacle of her career.

Despite the fact that she was no longer the feisty teen-ager of a few years past, Lotta retained her gamin-like acting routines, continuing to wear the enticingly short skirts of her innocent youth that gained her such popularity. Her childlike winsomeness allowed her to be risque but in a totally unoffending manner.

Having devoted her life to the theater, Lotta never had an enduring romance despite the many rumors published in the press of supposed love affairs with various male acquaintances. But none of these were serious relationships and Lotta never married.

After a career that had spanned nearly thirty-eight years, Lotta decided to retire at the peak of her fame, when she was only forty-four. Thanks to her mother's careful and watchful eye over her earnings, Lotta was a multi-millionaire and, despite the pleadings of many of her admirers, she never came out of retirement. She spent her time painting, a favorite hobby she had learned while visiting Paris. She eventually purchased a hotel in Boston which catered to actors and actresses and she spent time at a hideaway in New Jersey.

In 1875 Lotta saluted her California roots and presented the city of San Francisco with a twenty-four foot cast-iron monument which was placed at the corner of Market and Kearney streets in the heart of town. It is still standing, having survived the disastrous earthquake of 1906. It is a fitting tribute to one of the most popular and beloved Californians of all time.

THE DIARY OF LILLIE LANGTRY

Lotta Crabtree was one of a kind. Her legacy is that she made the lives of thousands of stage-goers happy with her ebullient, outgoing and delightful personality.

12

The Terrible Swift Sword
of Justice

*For all the beauty in the American West, its justice system
can be quick and severe when dealing out punishment for a
crime.*

Today was not a good day to arrive in Virginia City,
Nevada. I came here to appear in Piper's Opera
House, but found myself so ill from what I saw that
I have had to retire to my room to recover from the
sickening sight. The play will go on tonight, but my heart
will not be in it.

It seems that a woman named Julia Willis was murdered
by a wanderer and that this woman reminded the town of
another Julia. They hanged the killer of Julia Willis today,
just at the time of my arrival. Poor Beverly, he felt so badly
about it all that he, too, is lying with nausea in his room.
Thank God Freddie was not here, or he would also have
taken ill from the horrible sight of that man falling through
the trap door to his death.

The townspeople then told me it was very much like the
hanging of a man who murdered the most famous of all

Virginia City women, one called Julia Bulette, a woman who, ironically, was a native of London.

A thousand people were on hand for this hanging, and they sickened me when they cheered so wildly that they seemed more like a mob than a group of good citizens. They told me afterwards, however, that even more — ten thousand, they say — came for the hanging of the man who murdered Julia Bulette. They came from all over, just for the hanging and they cheered for days afterwards.

How can I tonight then, enjoy their applause? Do they not understand the difference between art and the execution of a man?

(Editor's note: The next page of Lillie's notes were too decayed to read. She continued with the following which appears to have been written the next day).

I do hope today that I shall feel better, for I plan to visit some property outside of town that I wish to purchase as an investment. It seems a good thing to me since so much gold and silver has been found in this area. Beverly just dropped by to tell me the coach will be ready in one hour. I am ready now. I think I will go outside and walk the streets to see what Virginia City is like on a quiet day.

I have visited the property I came to see and made an offer to buy it for very little money. I believe I shall be a Nevada property owner by the end of the morrow. There is no reason I cannot make a small fortune from my investment. I also learned more about Julia Bulette and feel her story should be told. It is worthy of Oscar turning it into a play or perhaps he would find it poetic. I will mail him the story as I write here, before I leave here.

My dearest Oscar,

I have a tale I need desperately to pass on to you, either because I believe the woman who is the center of the story was a remarkable human, or because the hanging I have just witnessed — of a man who murdered another woman — was so awfully sickening that I must purge myself of the depression it has put me into. I do hope I am not burdening you with this sad tale, and that maybe you will find something in the story to help others justify its meaning.

Julia Bulette was from London, although they tell me she did some growing up in New Orleans. Julia was remarkably strong willed and equally strong in body and, apparently, very beautiful. For instance, as for her strength, she saved Virginia City's life one week when the citizens were struck down by an epidemic. She went from tent to tent and house to house to administer medicine and to feed those who could eat — usually food that she herself prepared. She gave them hope with her presence and her aid. It didn't matter either if they were poor or rich people.

Julia was also the first to donate money and food to the widows of miners who died in the mines. She helped start and then always contributed to the local Sanitation Fund. *(Editor's note: The Sanitation Fund was the forerunner of the American Red Cross).* When Indians (known as Paiutes hereabouts) attacked the town, Julia refused to leave, instead staying to help nurse the men who were wounded.

Julia was so loved by the miners that they elected her an honorary member of their fire fighting group, the Virginia Engine Company Number One. They tell me that so far, no other woman in America has been so honored. The gentleman who drove the coach today told me that she loved the recognition and that she rode in every parade sitting atop the brass and silver fire engine. And when

Virginia City was nearly overcome by fire a few years ago, "Julia was the one who fed us and brought us coffee while we fought off the flames. Yes, sir," my driver said, "she was some strong woman."

Americans speak rather peculiarly at times, as you learned in Leadville, Colorado, but I find it to be a quaint honesty.

It sounds to me also that Julia might have liked my Lalee if she'd lived long enough to see it. The Truckee Railroad named a club car after her, calling it the *Julia Bulette*. And one of the Comstock mines was so named.

There is a knock at my door. I will continue this when I return.

Oscar, it is hours later and soon I must be at the Opera House for makeup and wardrobe. A group of local women dropped by and I am horrified to tell you that they have expressed some form of glee that Julia Bulette is no longer among them. These women were here twenty years ago when Julia was murdered. They still harbor hostility toward her, which for me is not understandable. They expressed to me that it was not ladylike for me to be asking questions about her while I visited the town. They very seriously want me to "drop the subject of Julia Bulette, because it can only rile the men up." What kind of people are these who wish others dead, and wish their memories dead with them? They remind me of your statement a few months back, "There is no sin but stupidity." Are these the sinners? Is Julia Bulette to be a martyr for something I have yet to learn?

The men have told me that Julia was a civic leader, a social leader as well. I have learned also that she had her own loge seat at the Opera House where she attended every play. But the women of Virginia City tell me otherwise. They say that Julia Bulette was a madam, a woman who "sold other women's flesh to the will of men." And dear Oscar, these women found it very, very difficult to express that opinion.

Contrast their description of her to the gentleman today who said clearly, "She may have been scarlet, but her heart was pure white."

You cannot find it written anywhere, but they called her place "Julia's Palace" and I am told it became a cultural retreat where fine wines and the best in French cooking made evenings delightful. She must have felt like royalty at times too, Oscar, because she rode around town in her own coach with her own crest emblazoned on the door. Once again, no pictures or newspaper articles to back that up, but the men all swear to it, and I have no reason to not believe them. The ladies however, decry these descriptions of Julia Bulette. Their scorn seems merely a sign of their pettiness.

One of her oldest and dearest friends was a local rancher named Cunningham. I met him today. He told me that he owned a mine in Bodie back then from which he took a lot of gold. He said, "At times I would drive a pair of fast geldings up the hill to Virginia City and throw a bunch of parties for Julia. Fabulous parties with music, dancing and lots of food." He told me he would give Julia a new diamond each time he did that, and for the other lady guests he gave sacks of gold dust.

There is no doubt Julia was a high-class madam. But she also carried a queenly air about her and she was known to be charming, full of good humor and showed excellent taste in foods and wines. At any rate, I have learned that Julia was given a fine funeral, one of the very best the Comstock has ever seen. One that clearly expressed the town's love for her, Mr. Cunningham told me. "There was a band, eighteen carriages and the men of the Virginia Engine Company Number One marching alongside her casket. We took her up to Flowery Hill Cemetery," he said proudly. I visited the cemetery today with him. He also informed me that she rests in a silver-handled coffin "which rode in a glass-walled hearse."

The women were not as kind. They told me just now, that they would have nothing to do with that funeral, that only men attended. "Unless, of course," one of them added, "they were the shady ladies who worked for her." One of the women said she marched to the parade and dragged her husband by the ear away from it.

Oh, have I told you, the name of Julia's killer was John Millain. He was a Frenchman. (Does that surprise you?) He claimed to be innocent, but the townspeople tell me they had "the goods on him."

Apparently, there were witnesses and he did have in his possession some of Julia's jewelry. They also found a trunk full of Julia's possessions in his quarters.

I am still disturbed by the visit of the three ladies of Virginia City a few moments ago. They seemed absolutely delighted that this Millain man killed Julia Bulette. I remember verbatim some of the things they just told me:

"It was a godsend that Millain got rid of our infamous painted lady."

"We took him all kinds of fancy food to his jail cell, just to say thank you."

"We tried to get the governor to commute his sentence."

They proceeded to show me picture postcards of Millain that were sold at his hanging. It was obviously turned into a commercial event.

One of the ladies also said, "He thanked us just before they hung him. Stood right up there on th platform and in perfect English, he thanked all the ladies of Virginia City for our concern and our food."

I find it amazing how criminals who are obviously guilty can play upon the emotions of people, such as the ladies who visited me, to the point where they become minor celebrities. The law officials I talked to said there was no doubt in their minds that Millain was the man who killed Julia Bulette. The evidence against him was just too strong. Yet these ladies seemed pleased he had committed a deed so foul and went so far as to try and get him released from prison. Granted, Julia may not have been the solid, upstanding citizen that others were, but in her own way she was probably as noble as any of them. Perhaps more so.

I can only sum it up by saying I am aghast at the goings on in this town.

Please come here and travel with me for a while. I miss you Oscar Wilde, you are the only man who seems to put sanity into all the right words.

Love, Lillie

Fortunately, as time passed, my opinion of Virginia City grew less severe and I less critical. People must do what they must do and who am I to pretend to sit in judgement of their actions?

13

Two Women of Tombstone

The West was truly unique. The men were a special breed and their women, while usually kept in the background, were just as distinctive. Yet their passions were the same as found anywhere in the world.

It was our custom when visiting the large cities and smaller hamlets of the United States to do as much sightseeing as time would allow. The contrast of American cities to those of Europe was one of the great attractions of the States. In many respects I found the Americans to be much further advanced in some basic human comforts, especially in the cosmopolitan cities of the East. For example, I seldom found a hotel in Europe that could rival those magnificent edifices that were going up all over the Eastern portion of the U.S., especially New York City.

As we traveled West, there was a notable decline in the comforts we had become used to in the East. This was to be expected. America was, of course, first settled on its Eastern coast so it stands to reason that cities like New York, Boston, Philadelphia and others of that area were far ahead of those to the West as far as development was concerned.

But Western cities from Chicago on to San Francisco were growing fast and furiously. It was when visiting the smaller towns that I found myself transposed into another era but one that was, nonetheless, equally as fascinating as the times I knew in the larger cities.

One of the most interesting places our troupe visited was the small but thriving town of Tombstone, in the Southern reaches of the Arizona Territory. While the name "Tombstone" is rather foreboding, I found the town, although small, to be bustling with miners, ranchers, cattle men and the usual host of gamblers who seemed to make it a point to be wherever an opportunity was presented to make a profit while plying their skills with playing cards.

While Tombstone was less than a major stop during our travels, it did provide me with one of the most memorable experiences during my many tours of the States. I became the reluctant arbiter in a bittersweet love affair and I shall try to recreate the incident now on these pages.

There was not much to see in Tombstone. It was like most of the smaller towns in the West as far as the casual observer could ascertain — dirt streets, hastily-constructed storefronts, some structures whose walls were surfaced with nothing stronger than canvas. But Tombstone had been the site of an incident that was not only well known in the West but apparently had been reported in news journals all over America. I must confess it was something of which I was not aware, but it was the talk of the town and I repeat it here in order to set the stage for what happened to me afterwards.

On October 27, 1881, there occurred in Tombstone the culmination of a feud that had been brewing between the Earp family — more specifically, the brothers Wyatt, Virgil and Morgan — and the Clanton clan, led by the brothers

Bill and Ike. Also involved in this event, on the side of the Earps, was one "Doc" Holliday, who, despite his proclivity for gambling and liquor, was indeed a legitimate dentist, as I found out later at another time and another place. But that is a story I will detail elsewhere.

The result of this feud in Tombstone was the death of Bill Clanton and two of his cohorts, the McLowry brothers. I am told the whole incident lasted but a matter of seconds and took place near the O.K. Corral.

Apparently the leader of the Earp clan was Wyatt, a lawman, Wells Fargo agent, sometime gambler and miner. We were shown the site of the incident and I must confess if I had not known it was where several men had met a violent death, I would not have been able to distinguish it from any other part of the small town. It was as we were leaving the area that my involvement in this rather distasteful affair began.

A woman approached me and upon looking into her eyes I could immediately tell she had been distraught for some time. She was young, probably in her mid twenties, but the years had not been kind to her. She was not unattractive, but she had a wild gaze in her eyes and while I cannot positively say that she was not in her right mind, she was undoubtedly a very troubled young woman. And not without reason, as I was soon to learn.

Her first words to me were, "Have you seen them?"

I had, of course, not the slightest idea as to whom she was referring.

"I beg your pardon, madam. Have I seen whom?" I responded.

Her eyes darted in all directions, as if she was frightened of being seen talking to me. Yet she persisted.

"Them! The two of them! They come here regularly now — with no shame at all," she said.

By now the rest of our group had moved on and were several paces ahead of me. Freddie, however, had seen the woman approach me and tarried a few feet away, now somewhat concerned with my safety. I did not feel threatened by the stranger because she made a pathetic sight and seemed harmless enough. I turned to her and said, "I must confess I do not know what you are talking about, madame. You must have me confused with someone else."

"Not at all, Mrs. Langtry," she replied. "I knew you were in town and I must talk to you."

I glanced toward Freddie, who had a quizzical look on his face, much the same as did I. The woman now seemed steadier and in better control of herself.

"My name is Celia Ann," she said. "But they call me Mattie. Mattie Earp."

Now that last name, of course, suddenly rang a bell. "Earp," I replied. "Are you related to..."

Before I could finish, she interrupted. "I am the wife of Wyatt Earp."

Suddenly things were beginning to fall together, although I was still somewhat befuddled over this impromptu meeting. "It was Mr. Earp who was involved in the recent..."

I was at a loss for a specific word to describe the event.

"Shootout," she said. "But that's not the reason I must talk to you, Mrs. Langtry."

"Well, Mattie, you certainly have my attention. How can I be of help?"

"You're an educated woman, Mrs. Langtry. You've been all over the world, seen and done things that I will never do even in my wildest dreams. I am simply the wife of Wyatt

122

Earp. I dutifully came with him to this godforsaken place when he left Dodge City. I have lived with him and the rest of the Earp clan and tried to be a good woman for him, and look what he's done to me!"

At first I had no idea to what she was referring, thinking possibly that she was upset over the "shootout," as she called it. "Exactly what is it that has you so upset, Mattie," I asked. "What *has* Mr. Earp done to you?"

"He's run off with another woman, that's what!" she exclaimed, her eyes blazing in anger.

Now it suddenly dawned on me what was troubling Mattie. The age old problem of a woman scorned.

"And what's more," she said, "he won't even acknowledge me. It's like I didn't even exist, even though we're still living in the same household. Do you know what he did after the shootout, Mrs. Langtry? He came home and without so much as a word to me, went to see that other woman. He went to visit that hussy! Can you imagine? And me with my heart in my mouth, not knowing whether he was dead at the hands of those terrible Clantons or what!"

I could not do much to assuage the grief Mattie was feeling and I do think she was looking to me as a neutral ear who would listen to her unburden herself rather than someone who could solve what really was an insoluble problem.

"It is difficult to understand what makes people act the way they do when it comes to affairs of the heart," I said to her, trying as best I could to offer her a small bit of verbal comfort.

"Don't be swayed by what you hear," Mattie warned me. I did not try to explain to her that my stay in Tombstone would be so brief that it was unlikely I would talk to anyone

123

outside my own group of actors, but in this regard I was mistaken.

At the theater that night, I was approached by none other than *the other woman* in this triangle. Her name was Josephine Sarah Marcus, and as if I had been designated the grand arbiter in the love affairs of one Wyatt Earp, she told me the story from her point of view.

Wyatt Earp arrived in Tombstone in December of 1879. Josephine reluctantly admitted that Mattie was with him, although she maintains they were not legally married but merely living together as man and wife. Wyatt, she told me, was married in 1870 in Lamar, Missouri, to Urilla Sutherland. Unfortunately, Urilla died later that year during childbirth. The poor child did not survive, either. It is my belief that Wyatt never married officially again. I doubt that he and Maggie were legally married and the same holds true for his relationship with Josephine. But I am getting ahead of my story.

According to Josephine, Mattie did come to Tombstone with the Earp clan, as she told me, and she was only twenty-two at the time. But, while she lived with the Earps, Maggie's relationship with Wyatt had totally diminished to one of a housekeeper and Wyatt had lost any feelings of love he once might have had for her.

"She had a terrible temper," Josephine maintained, speaking of Mattie. "It was a wonder Wyatt stayed with her as long as he did. It was more out of pity than anything else, because Wyatt is a truly wonderful and respectful man," she added.

I asked Josephine how she happened to come to Tombstone because, with my actresses' ear, I detected an Eastern accent in her voice. She told me that her family indeed had come from New York, where she was born, and eventually settled in San Francisco. Her father, a German Jew, was a successful businessman, and while still in school Josephine was smitten with the theater and ran away from home to join the touring company of *H. M. S. Pinafore.*

She came with the company to Tombstone in 1880, shortly after the Earps had arrived and, at the time she was in love with Johnny Behan, a local law official, whom she had planned to marry. Curiously, it was Behan who introduced Josephine to Wyatt Earp. While the two men eventually became mortal enemies, they were at the time on friendly terms and Josephine soon found herself falling in love with Earp. Behan was sheriff of Tombstone when the Earps confronted the Clantons and one wonders if there was a jealousy motive involved in Wyatt and Behan's eventual falling out.

Exactly when Josephine and Wyatt began their affair is hard to pinpoint. One thing I found in talking on separate occasions to both Mattie and Josephine was their reluctance to be specific about certain important details. While I doubt very much that the goings on at Tombstone will be of much historical significance as the years go by, I feel sorry for any historians who will attempt to sort out the details of what transpired in this speck of a town near the Arizona-Mexican border.

I can only relate the story as it happened to me and cannot verify any of the incidents except to say I am reporting them exactly as they were told to me.

Mattie said it was no secret that Wyatt was seeing another woman while in Tombstone. He would ignore her and, although she was living with his family, tend to be very secretive about his relationship with her. Keep in mind that Mattie insists that she and Wyatt Earp were man and wife, although she was very evasive when I asked her for details about when and where they were married.

Josephine's affair with Wyatt apparently was not a great secret to the residents of Tombstone. Wyatt and Josephine were often seen together in public. Again, details were hard to extract from the two Earp women. Josephine at first told me she was living in a house owned by Johnny Behan, then she said she moved in with some friends. Mattie maintains that Josephine was nothing more than a working prostitute, but this statement must be taken for what it is worth, considering the source was a woman who hated Josephine.

One thing I concluded from talking to both women was that Wyatt definitely had chosen Josephine over Mattie. It is quite apparent why he was intrigued by Josephine. She was exotically beautiful, with dark eyes and an exquisite figure which she emphasized by the outfits she wore. Mattie, on the other hand, while pleasant-looking enough in a plain way, was slightly roundfaced and not especially well clothed although in her defense it must be said that when I met her she was totally distraught over her broken love affair with Wyatt Earp.

How this love triangle was eventually resolved among the participants was certainly no doing of mine because I was in Tombstone for less than forty-eight hours. Wyatt was having legal problems over the incident near the O.K. Corral, although he was absolved of any blame by a local court. Sadly, the shootout ignited a vendetta by both parties, and Wyatt's younger brother, Morgan, was shot and killed by one of the Clanton gang seeking revenge. It is said that in retaliation Wyatt sought after the killer and eventually gunned him down. When someone dubbed it "The Wild West," it was undoubtedly incidents such as these they were referring to. There is no part of the world quite like Western America where you can be in a cultured, civilized city today and tomorrow be in a land overrun by cattle rustlers, gun-toting cowboys, Indians on the warpath and gamblers who would shoot you at the drop of a Faro card. But this is what made my travels in America exciting and I wouldn't have chanced to miss those days for anything in the world. It was a far cry from the salons of Europe and the civility of London and Paris but a once in a lifetime experience.

Wyatt Earp left Tombstone in March of 1882 after a brief stay of twenty-seven months in the town. There is no doubt, however, that his exploits there will long be remembered by the local citizenry. However, in the greater scheme of things, they will not likely survive much beyond the story-tellers of that small Arizona hamlet.

Josephine went with Wyatt. It is my understanding they are still together to this day. As for Mattie, her story is a sad one. Abandoned by Wyatt, she drifted to other towns in the area, eventually turning to prostitution in order to make her way. I have detailed in another section of this tome how difficult it was for women to obtain legitimate jobs during that period in the West. Suffice it here to say that Mattie had little choice but to turn to "the world's oldest profession."

To escape her memories she also took to drink. In 1888, while in Pinal, Arizona Territory, Mattie was found dead in her bed. The official cause of her death was listed as suicide, but it seems more appropriate to me to say that Mattie died of a broken heart.

So ends the story as I know it of Tombstone, Wyatt, Mattie and Josephine Earp. I pass it on here not because it is of any historical import, but mainly because it shows that affairs of the heart, while maybe simple on the surface, are in reality complicated and complex.

Lillie Langtry

Lillie on Stage

Albert Edward, Prince of Wales
before he became King Edward VII

Oscar Wilde

Lotta Crabtree

Jessie Fremont

Judge Roy Bean and his saloon-courthouse,
the "Jersey Lily" in Langtry, Texas.

Lola Montez

Dr. Bethenia Owens

Ogarita Booth

General A. E. Burnside

Susan Elston Wallace

Lew Wallace

Sarah Bernhardt

Helen Modjeska

"Doc" Holliday

Kate Elder

Belle Starr

"Baby Doe" Tabor

Olive Oatman

Dr. Mary Walker

Celia Ann "Mattie" Blaylock

Josephine Sarah Marcus

Wyatt Earp

Bat Masterson

14

The Six Thousand Mile Meeting

The unexpected has occurred so persistently in my life that I am no longer surprised at any event in which I am involved. A chance meeting with an old acquaintance some six thousand miles from my home in England can only be attributed to a pleasant coincidence.

My property in Bournemouth, sometimes called The Red House, located at the corner of Derby Road and Knyveton Road, it turns out, was not far from the home of Sir Percy and Lady Shelley. Sir Percy was the only surviving son of the poet Shelley and Mary Wollstonecraft Shelley, she being the authoress of that somewhat frightening novel, *Frankenstein or The Modern Prometheus*.

Sir Percy and Lady Shelley were quite friendly neighbors, and, in fact, he was an amateur playwright and built the first theater in Bournemouth. It is said his intentions were somewhat self-serving, because Sir Percy used the theater to produce his own works, although I was never asked by him to appear in any of his plays, the reason being, I am told, that he felt it improper to ask me, a professional, when all his actors and he, himself, in fact, were amateurs.

What my reply might have been it is difficult to say, the question never having been asked, although in retrospect I can see no harm in performing for him, especially since any income derived was used for charitable contributions. But I drift from the point of my tale.

It seems the Shelley's were friendly with a young man who was to earn quite a reputation for himself as a successful novelist, and it is my chance meeting with him in England which led to a reunion some thousands of miles away that makes one realize that this earth of ours is not such a large place after all.

As was my usual regimen, I was out at dawn this day to run my two miles which, while perhaps not too ladylike, I insist on doing to maintain good health. This most interesting young man was sitting just outside the gate to the Shelley estate, writing in a tablet as I came by. He stood, smiled, and tipped his hat to me and bid me a friendly good morning. I slowed, then finally stopped since I was quite near home, and acknowledged his greeting. He was a reasonably attractive man, but far from healthy looking. Rather gaunt and pale, he was nonetheless a gentleman with a great deal of charm.

"Forgive me, Mrs. Langtry," he said, "but I am a great admirer of yours. My name is Robert Louis Stevenson."

"Thank you, sir," I responded, "And I have been a great admirer of yours since reading your first novel, *An Inland Voyage*."

"Indeed?" he replied, a surprised look coming over his face. "I am doubly honored to think the great beauty of our age has read one of my works."

"Will these compliments between us never cease?" I said, smiling in an attempt to put him at ease. "Are you a guest of Sir Percy and Lady Shelley?" I inquired.

"Yes, on a somewhat regular basis, actually. I had heard you were a neighbor, but not a regular resident of The Red House," Stevenson said.

"Unfortunately that is true," I answered. "It is not by choice that I am away so many days of the year, but my acting keeps me on the road much more than I like," I told him.

It was time to move along, and as we bade each other good-day, Stevenson told me, "A confession, beautiful lady. I heard that you took your exercise each morning at dawn and I was determined to awaken early enough this day in order to meet you. Forgive my impertinence, but for me it was a pleasure I shall never forget."

I smiled and thanked him for his kind words. Writers, I have learned from dear Oscar Wilde, have a profound way of saying nice things.

I later learned that Stevenson had been in Bournemouth in an attempt to improve his nagging health problems. My initial observation was correct when he impressed me as a man who was not well. Indeed, he had spent time in the South of France, Switzerland and now, Bournemouth, hoping to rid himself of a persistent cough.

I did not see him again in Bournemouth because I was soon off again on tour, eventually traveling to America and thence across the great breadth of that enormous country, where my troupe and I gave performances in most major and minor cities.

We eventually arrived in the Westernmost part of the U.S., the state of California which, as I have noted in previous entries in this diary, is a land of sunshine, beauty and charm. It was here that fate, that strange, unpredictable lady, stepped in and I was to meet up with Robert Louis Stevenson once again.

THE DIARY OF LILLIE LANGTRY

The Lalee was going North toward San Francisco, but we had scheduled a stop in the town of Monterey, some 100 miles to the South of the city by the Golden Gate. We would give an evening performance there and had arrived a day early in order to rehearse a new play that we would eventually debut in San Francisco. As was the case in all the cities I visited, members of the press would gather at the station in order to interview me. Although this was a somewhat tiring procedure, it was a necessary one, and goodness knows the same questions were asked so many times that I did not need any rehearsal time for my answers.

Imagine my surprise when a voice from the crowd of admirers that had gathered around the Lalee had a decided British accent although the reporter identified himself as working for the *Monterey Californian,* the local newspaper.

"Mrs. Langtry," he said, "How are things at dear old Bournemouth?"

I strained my neck to see who it was and who should I observe in the crowd but the smiling face of Robert Louis Stevenson. Thinner than ever, in a suit of clothes that looked as if it had been slept in more than once (which, indeed, it had), Stevenson stepped from the crowd and approached me as I beckoned for him to come closer.

"Mr. Stevenson!" I said, hardly concealing my surprise.

He smiled and took my outstretched hand. "We have both traveled some many miles since we last saw each other in England," he said.

"Yes," I replied, "and I must confess while I know why *I* am here, I have no idea at all what brings you so many thousands of miles from home."

"Love," Mrs. Langtry, "plain and simple, it's love."

Now it is no secret that I am a romanticist, so needless to say, Mr. Stevenson's reply piqued my interest.

"I have followed the love of my life across the continents to seek her hand in marriage."

For a moment I wondered if Mr. Stevenson had taken leave of his senses — surely he was not talking about me, was he? Then he quickly explained.

"Her name is Frances Matilda Osbourne — Fanny, I call her," he told me. "She's an American. We met in France while she was studying art. Unfortunately, she is married."

"Oh, dear," I said. "This sounds like it could be a trip that was made in vain."

"Not so. Her husband has agreed to give her a divorce — they're much easier to get in the States than they are in our country, Mrs. Langtry."

How well I knew that to be true. For years Mr. Langtry had refused my request for a divorce even though we had not been living as man and wife for more time than I care to reveal. My lawyers have been trying to get me American citizenship papers in order to facilitate a divorce, but while they think they will be successful in the long run, that is another story for another day. Suffice it to say here and now that Robert Louis Stevenson was apparently going to be able to marry his true love.

"I am very happy for you, Mr. Stevenson," I told him and I was sincere in saying that. The poor man looked quite decrepit and I was to learn later that he had been quite wretched in California, oftentimes sleeping on a dirt floor and having barely enough money to sustain himself. His illness was undiagnosed at the time, but he wrote to a friend that it was "a toss-up for life or death" and by his appearance I would agree.

It was an attempt to earn a few pennies that he took the job of freelance writing for the *Californian*. If only the editors of that journal knew that they had one of the great writers of the age working for them they most likely would have treated him with more respect.

"I am a happy man, Mrs. Langtry," Mr. Stevenson told me. "Fanny and I will be married in San Francisco in mid-May. Do stop in and see us if you find the time."

"I will certainly try," I replied.

"Meanwhile," he said, "it's back to the business at hand. May I write an article about two countrymen meeting some six thousand miles from their homeland?"

"I would be honored," I told him.

Robert Louis Stevenson smiled and waved goodbye as the crowd closed in on me. I was sorry I didn't think to ask him for dinner, but he disappeared into the crowd so quickly it was not possible. I never saw him again, but I made it a point to follow his life's story as closely as I could.

He did indeed marry the love of his life, Fanny, the American woman who was ten years older than he. She nursed him back to good health but it is said the poor soul had to have all his teeth removed in order to rid his body of an infection that had been coursing through it.

Mr. Stevenson's parents were quite opposed to the marriage but, fortunately, they later reconciled and he brought Fanny home to Scotland to meet them. She was a loyal and devoted wife and he a loving husband and adoring father to her two children. In fact, he collaborated with his son, Samuel Lloyd Osbourne, on three books — *The Wrong Box*, *The Ebb-Tide* and *The Wrecker*.

Fanny's life with Mr. Stevenson was not an easy one. His ailment, eventually diagnosed as tuberculosis, continued to trouble him and she spent much of her time caring for him.

In one of his writings after having been married for a few years, he wrote: "Marriage is one long conversation, chequered by disputes. The disputes are valueless; they but ingrain the difference; the heroic heart of woman prompting her at once to nail her colours to the mast. But in the intervals, almost unconsciously and with no desire to shine, the whole material of life is turned over and over, ideas are struck out and shared, the two persons more and more adapt their notions one to suit the other, and in process of time, without sound of trumpets, they conduct each other into new worlds of thought."

I do believe Mr. and Mrs. Stevenson were a happily married couple. I find it interesting and another coincidence that the Stevenson's honeymooned by taking the train through Napa and St. Helena, spending some time at the resort village of Calistoga, all three sites being relatively near the ranch I was to purchase near Middletown.

The couple eventually traveled to Saranac Lake in New York where the renowned Dr. E. L. Trudeau told Mr. Stevenson that his disease was arrested. He continued to be troubled, however, and eventually his world travels took him to the South Pacific in a chartered yacht. He, along with Fanny, his mother and son, visited the Marquesas, Tuamotu, Tahiti, Hawaii, Micronesia and Australia. What a great adventure for the brilliant writer!

Eventually, the Stevensons bought property in Samoa, where they built a permanent home which he named Vailima (Five Streams). He became very active with the natives and they looked upon him as a great friend and supporter. There, in Samoa, many thousands of miles from his native England, Robert Louis Stevenson spent some of the most joyful days of his life. His beloved Fanny was continually with him until he died, unexpectedly, on December 3, 1894, being only forty-four years old.

He was buried high atop a hill on his lovely Samoan estate and I am told the natives treat the location with great respect and reverence. They knew Robert Louis Stevenson not as we of the Western world did, as a great and talented author, but more as a man of peace and tranquility who settled in their land and became a great believer in their ways and traditions. That he was able to make what must have been a tremendous adjustment for a man born and raised so many thousands of miles away and in such a different culture, speaks highly not only of Stevenson, but of the Samoans he grew to love and respect.

Luckily for the rest of us, Robert Louis Stevenson lived long enough to produce some of the greatest literature of our age. Who will ever forget his novels like *Treasure Island,* or *The Strange Case of Dr. Jekyll and Mr. Hyde,* or his lilting poems in *A Child's Garden of Verses?* And what about the thrilling *Kidnapped* and its sequel, *David Balfour?* Then there was *The Master of Ballentrae* and *The Black Arrow* and so many others.

Oftentimes I will reach for my first-edition copy of *Treasure Island,* in which Mr. Stevenson admits to having incorporated portions of scenic California in its pages. I smile as I think of our first visit in England and then how we met again in Monterey, so many, many miles away. From the many letters both he and Fanny sent me, I feel certain his short life was a happy one.

I was once asked who was the most brilliant writer I had ever known. Was it Oscar Wilde — Robert Louis Stevenson — Lew Wallace — or perhaps someone else? Needless to say, this is an impossible question for me to answer. It is best that I let history be the judge and I rejoice in having known such talented men.

15

Calamity at The
East Lynne Opera House

I have encountered a woman I ultimately found to be pathetic, distasteful and unfortunately, theatrically stimulating, even though misguided. I am compelled to write down the events that lead me to my emotions concerning this woman.

Montana is one of the most beautiful places I have ever seen in the summer. The mountains are spectacular, especially those North of Missoula and Kalispell, near the Blackfoot Indian reservation. These glacier peaks have snow on them even during the warm summer months.

The hills and valleys of this part of Montana are alive with rich green trees and brush. Rivers flow freely and wildly for miles in all directions. There is abundant wildlife always in view including geese, deer and even mountain lions — beautiful large cats one must not fear but must at the same time respect cautiously.

We came to Virginia City, Montana, through Bozeman, where the Lalee was left behind after a rather arduous trip across Eastern Montana, which appears to be a vast open grazing land for buffalo, elk and deer. A private coach that Beverly was able to obtain for us, although it's still a method of travel I do not very much like, took us the rest of the way.

I find it confusing that America has so many cities with the same name like Virginia City, Nevada, and Virginia City, Montana. There's also Nevada City, California, and once again, just north of here, there is Nevada City, Montana. But I drift from my main story.

I was not in town but an hour when I met her.

She told me her real name was Martha Jane Canarray, but that she went by "Calamity Jane."

When I asked her why, she only grinned back. Little did I understand that by that same evening, I would be able to see for myself the reason.

Jane looked very much like a man when I met her in front of the hotel. She sauntered up to me, a pistol attached to her left hip in such a way she would have to pull it out with her right hand, just like many of the cowboys here in America wear them, and said, "You must be that actress lady."

"I am an actress," I said. I smiled, hoping that would ease her, because I thought she might be shy or nervous. But I was wrong. "My name is Lillie Langtry," I told her.

"Howdy, Langtry. I was an actress once," she said.

"Is that true?"

"Yep. Back in Deadwood. Black Hills country. The Dakotas."

"You're from there?"

She laughed, then expectorated tobacco out into the street. I find this habit among cowboys abhorrent, so when I saw it coming from a woman you can understand why I stepped back and involuntarily placed my hand over my mouth. Jane shouted out for everyone to hear, "Heck no, lady. I'm from here. Born and raised. I got to Deadwood 'cause I joined up with General Crook back in '75 as a scout in the Black Hills. Injuns, don't you know. Married Wild Bill Hickok I did."

By then I wanted to get away from this woman who wore pants and chaps, a heavy wool shirt and a man's hat. She appeared so much like a cowboy I wasn't sure she was a woman. I hasten to add, and please forgive me, that she even *smelled* like a cowboy.

"Well, it's been nice meeting you Jane, but I must retire before the play this evening. You know how important rest is to actresses."

She laughed, and said, "You bet. Get some sleep, Langtry. I'll see you tonight, front row center."

True to her word, Jane was there during the show, exactly where she said she'd be — front row and center seats. She had brought a gunslinger friend along with her. He was tough looking and like so many I have seen here, ready to draw and fire at a moment's notice. The play was one of my favorites, but apparently not one of Jane's. She became enraged toward the end from something we were doing — I never did learn what — and stood straight up in her seat and started shouting and yelling. Then she let loose a long stream of tobacco juice toward the stage. It almost hit me! How disgusting.

Her gunslinger friend jumped up and whooped and hollered and started shooting out all the lamps. The audience went wild with delight. Can you believe that? They cheered and laughed and clapped while Calamity Jane and her friend tore up the Opera House and destroyed our production.

When they were finished with their terror, they left us, arm in arm, marching straight up the aisle to the cheers of the crowd and out the front door.

The sheriff never made a move to stop them — and, I later learned, he was sitting in the second row aisle seat during the entire affair.

The following day her gunslinger friend was killed at the local bank by the same sheriff while the gunslinger was attempting to rob the bank. Calamity immediately left town. That was good, because I thought I never wanted to see Calamity Jane again.

But, a few years later, curiosity got the better of me.

We stopped in Deadwood, South Dakota, for a rest during our trip to St. Paul. It wasn't until I was in town for an hour that I recalled that Jane told me Deadwood was the town where she worked as an actress. I asked about her and the station master informed me that he had just heard she "was down the road in Terry," a small town just south of Deadwood.

I went there, against my best judgment. Insatiable curiosity has always been one of my weaknesses.

I found her in a rundown shack where she had lived the past year. She was much older looking, although she was still young.

She told me that after leaving Virginia City, she drifted through one Western town after another, making a few dollars here and there but never enough to "buy new clothes or feed myself well." She married several times, but they only lasted "a few days."

She got "so old looking, that my friends don't recognize me no more." So, she said, she wrote a short autobiography and began selling that for twenty-five cents a copy. (I have a copy that I will cherish for a long time). In her book she calls herself the "White Devil of the Yellowstone," but no matter where she went, people would shout, "Here comes Calamity Jane." She was not able to cast out her life-long reputation.

So she signed on with a traveling show and toured the Midwest, taking her rip-roaring life to the stage just as she had lived it. "But I always got drunk and then got fired," she explained. "I don't know why, but I just can't leave fire water alone."

She told me she had a daughter by Wild Bill Hickok. When I pressed her on this matter, she confessed the girl was really fathered by an army lieutenant, a man named Summers, a man she "ran around with for a while." She doesn't know where the daughter is — and I would not be surprised that she does not exist at all, although I am not one to doubt another woman's tale about a daughter when I have kept my own such a secret.

Jane became deathly ill about that time, but a bawdy house madam nursed her back to health. After that she was hired by the Pan American Exposition and paid very well to do her show again. "But there ya go again," she told me, "liquor did me in." She got drunk and started shooting her six shooters at Irish policemen who she made do the jig around her dancing bullets. She was run out of town.

After my visit with her, I could only muster sympathy in my heart for the poor woman. She was stretched out in a hovel, lying in a dirty little room where she was dying. She had led a wild, at times exciting although always senseless and useless life — and now she was to pay the ultimate price.

She had one last request. I passed it on to those who cared for her. She wanted to be buried next to Wild Bill Hickok, on Mt. Motiah, overlooking the town of Deadwood.

Her wishes were granted. I understand her funeral was the grandest funeral ever held in Deadwood for a woman.

Calamity Jane was known to the public as a wild, gun-toting, drunken woman. But in Deadwood they felt differently about her. She was a "saint" according to some, "a woman who cared for others, although she swore with the tongue of a bushwhacker while she did so." Proof came with a man who she had nursed back to health in his youth, when the smallpox epidemic took so many lives in Deadwood many years before. He closed her coffin.

And forever sealed Calamity Jane's haunting life with her.

While I was outraged at Jane's ill manners when I first met her, in retrospect I now realize she was doing the best she could in life under difficult circumstances.

16

The Governor
and His Wife

Truly, some men are gifted beyond mortals, it would seem. And how does a wife keep in stride with such a human being?

I think that during my first five-year stay in the United States I must have played every city, large and small, in that wonderful land. And I do believe I met some of the most colorful personalities anyone could possibly have the pleasure of knowing during that and subsequent tours.

My reputation, I say in all modesty, preceded me wherever I went and opened doors that would unlikely not have been as friendly had I not been blessed with the publicity that I seemed to generate.

We had just finished a tour of California and were headed East when we received a wire from Governor Lew Wallace beseeching us to alter our plans and add a few days' worth of performances in his Territory of New Mexico. As it turned out, it was not difficult inasmuch as we already had planned to divert our course somewhat, thanks to the cooperation of the Southern Pacific Railway, so we could visit the town in Texas named in my honor — Langtry. More about that interesting adventure later.

I agreed to make a stop in New Mexico and wired ahead to Governor Wallace that we would be pleased to present *She Stoops To Conquer* in the territorial capital of Santa Fe. I quickly admonished the protests of some of my troupe who much preferred playing the larger cities by reminding them that they had already performed in Leadville, which one newspaper journalist wrote is "Forty degrees nearer hell than any city in the Union." Having made my point, we proceeded across the vast desert in California, through Arizona Territory and finally into New Mexico.

Life in the West at that time, especially in the smaller towns and hamlets, was not easy. The men were strong, and, oftentimes, rough-edged by necessity. So the contrast in meeting a cultured gentleman who would have been at home in the fine salons of Europe in the wilds of New Mexico was even more startling than if I had met him, say, in a city like New York, Philadelphia or Boston.

Governor Wallace received me in his office soon after our arrival. He was a stately looking gentleman and is best described in a letter written by one Mary Clemmer who, I suspect, was enamored of the man, yet had the foresight to introduce him to his wife to be, Susan Arnold Elston. It was Susan Wallace who kindly let me read the description of her husband when he was a young man, as written to her by Miss Clemmer, to wit:

"He is fashioned of the refined clay of which nature is most sparing, nearly six feet high, perfectly straight, with a fine fibered frame all nerve and muscle, and so thin that he cannot weigh more than a hundred and thirty pounds.

"He has profuse black hair, a dark, beautiful face, correct in every line, keen black eyes deeply set, with a glance that on occasion may cut like fine steel. Black beard and mustache conceal the firm mouth and chin. His modest, quiet manner is the only *amende* that can be made for being so handsome. In a crowd anywhere you would single him out as a king of men."

Is it any wonder that Susan fell in love with this wonderful man and soon became his wife? It is an enduring love story that I feel privileged to have heard first hand from the lovely Mrs. Wallace.

But let me here tell more about this amazing man — and his equally amazing wife.

Governor Wallace was born in the state of Indiana in 1827 in what at that time was called the Western part of America but which more correctly is best described as being in the middle section of the country. A relatively new member of the Union when Governor Wallace was born, Indiana had been a state for only eleven years. But the Wallace family could trace its origins in the region back to his grandfather, who lived in Pennsylvania and later in Ohio. Governor Wallace's father, David, graduated from the U.S. Military Academy at West Point, New York, then, in 1821, resigned from the army and became a lawyer — a course that his son was to mirror some years later.

Young Lew Wallace grew up in Indiana and one of the major accomplishments of his young life was being taught to read by an Irish schoolteacher. Soon he was addicted to reading any book he could get his hands on. Another parallel in his life with his own father's was the fact that the senior Wallace preceded his son in a governorship, being elected governor of the state of Indiana in 1837. The Wallace family moved to the state capital, a village mainly inhabited by Indians which was called, appropriately enough, Indianapolis.

It was while residing in Indianapolis that young Wallace developed another of his many talents, that of drawing and painting. And while he never pursued art as a career, there is no doubt he would have been quite successful, for a study of his drawings reveal the work of a true professional.

The senior Wallace continued to be immersed in politics. Following his tenure as governor, he served a term in the U.S. Congress, then became a judge, a position he held until his death in 1859.

Young Lew was sent to live with an aunt in 1840, and continued to show an increasing interest in literary activities. He wrote poetry and even finished a novel entitled *The Man-at-Arms: A Tale of the Tenth Century* while still in his teens.

But the future governor had a wild streak in him and proved to be so uncontrollable that his father finally decided it was best if Lew leave the household and fend for himself. He soon found work in a law office but continued writing, his first love, although he realized an aspiring writer had to eat and earn enough for his lodgings, so he was careful to put in a full day's and some night work at the law firm.

Lew Wallace got his first official taste of the military when he joined the Indianapolis militia during the war with Mexico. While studying for the bar examination, he was more intrigued by the chance of army duty, and at the age of 19 he became a lieutenant and served on active duty during that war. There is no doubt his first hand vision of the horrors of war soon diminished any romantic notions he might have had about military life, but he was a strong supporter nevertheless of America's war with Mexico. Ironically, one of the results of the conflict was the acquisition of New Mexico by the United States, a territory that

Wallace would govern some thirty years later. But much happened in between those two events.

While Governor Wallace was still to participate in some of the major events of the century, I hasten to point out here that one of the milestones of his life occurred in 1848. This was the year he met his future wife, the aforementioned Susan Arnold Elston. Susan was the younger sister of Mrs. Henry S. Lane and Mr. Lane was a former army lieutenant colonel who was Lew Wallace's commanding officer during the Mexican War. Susan had been made aware of the future Governor Wallace in the letter written by Mary Clemmer, a letter Mrs. Wallace treasures to this day.

It was a romance of which novels are inspired. And one that has long endured, I am happy to say. More than fifty years after that first meeting, Governor Wallace wrote, "I can blow the time aside lightly as smoke from a cigar, and have a return of that evening with Miss Elston, and her blue eyes, wavy hair, fair face, girlish manner, delicate person, and witty flashes to vivify it." How romantic. And when he and Susan were celebrating their golden wedding anniversary, Governor Wallace would not accept the idea that "a man past seventy may not be moved by the love of his youth."

But wooing and winning Susan's hand did not come easily. Her wealthy and influential father was not particularly impressed by the young man and there were several other suitors to contend with. Obviously, Susan's hand was well worth winning. Inspired now by true love, young Wallace immersed himself into his law studies in earnest and in 1849 passed the bar and became a full-fledged lawyer.

Young Mr. Wallace set up his law practice in his boyhood hometown of Covington and one must wonder if the location of the office was not so much attributed to nostalgia but rather to the fact that it was only a reasonable distance from Susan's home in Crawfordsville.

Because of the great number of lawyers in the area, budding barrister Wallace found business to be dismal at best. But determined to succeed — I like to think he was inspired by his love for Susan — he eventually was able to make ends meet and even earn some respect from Susan's parents, although they still had not been won over by him completely. But love conquers all. Lew Wallace — who called Susan in a letter to his brother "the greatest girl living" — and Susan were married on May 6, 1852. It was a marriage that was to endure for fifty-three years. In writing (in the third person) about his wife some years after their marriage, he said, "Probably no man, in his efforts to achieve renown, was ever better seconded by his wife...Her culture, taste, and criticism must have been invaluable to him...He is an artist, and for pastime has covered his walls with pictures; and as they are both tireless readers, books have overflowed the whole house. Visitors who enter their doors, and look upon their lives, come away assured that it is possible for man and wife to be extremely literary, and at the same time live in constant domestic happiness — possible for a woman to write poetry, and yet understand the whole art and mystery of housekeeping."

There was enough adventure ahead for the Wallaces to fill the lives of several men and women. I will touch only upon the highlights here, lest I devote an entire book to this remarkable man and his equally remarkable wife.

Continuing to build his law practice, the future governor continued with his love for writing and, in fact, completed the first draft of a novel entitled *The Fair God*. It is interesting to note, however, that Susan preceded him as a published author, having written a collection of poems, one of which, *The Patter of Little Feet*, earned her a reputation as a successful authoress.

The clouds of the great American civil conflict were beginning to gather and lawyer Wallace became more and more involved in politics, supporting Stephen Douglas for the presidency in the election of 1860. When Abraham Lincoln won the election, Lew Wallace, who had attended one of the Lincoln-Douglas debates, soon realized that he had favored the wrong man. Lincoln, he now felt, was the man who truly could lead the nation on the path of freedom for all.

It was on April 13, 1861 that Fort Sumter was fired upon, thus launching the terrible war between the states. President Lincoln called for the state of Indiana to furnish six regiments for the Union forces and Wallace, a veteran of the Mexican War, was soon organizing the necessary forces. I do not mean to slight his most impressive military record but, in the interest of space, let me say here that he became a Major General and was commander of the Union forces in the now-famous Battle of Shiloh.

But that still is not the end of Governor Wallace's large contribution to the historical events of the century. After the tragic assassination of President Lincoln, then General Wallace was among the members of the military tribunal which tried and convicted the conspirators who were captured after the dastardly event. And, probably because of his experience at that trial, he was appointed to head the military commission that would try Captain Henry Wirz, commander of the infamous Andersonville prison.

The saga — and indeed, that is not too strong a word to describe this man's life — of Lew Wallace continues. Concurrent with his other Civil War duties, he worked to help Benito Juarez, who freed Mexico from French domination.

Following the war he returned to his law practice, devoting much of his time aiding claims by Civil War veterans. It was in 1878 that he was appointed governor of the territory of New Mexico, and it was in this Southwest corner of the U.S. that I had the privilege of meeting and performing for Governor Wallace and his lovely wife, Susan.

I must now tell you about another interesting event in this man's unbelievable career. And I can report this first hand, because I was there when it happened. In fact, the Governor pointed out afterwards that it probably would not even have taken place except for me, although he may have been gallantly exaggerating somewhat. In any case, the Governor sponsored an exquisite dinner party and ball after our final performance in Santa Fe. It rivaled the best I have attended anywhere in the States. After dinner, while the men were gathered in the library in order to smoke their favorite cigars, there was a ruckus in the room and soon after several armed members of the Governor's militia were seen escorting a rather young but unkempt man out of the room in no uncertain fashion. I learned afterward that the young man had been in and out of trouble with the law, but that the Governor had agreed to offer him clemency if he would divulge what he knew about a certain Lincoln County "war." In reconstructing this event some years after the fact I find my mind a bit cloudy as to the exact details, but suffice it to say the young man was intent on discussing the matter with Governor Wallace in person and realized that the gathering in my honor would be a likely time to find the Governor without having to go through a maze of underlings.

I am told that the Governor was true to his word with the young man but that the territory's attorney general would not cooperate with the terms the Governor had agreed to. I do not know what became of the young man, but I do remember his name to this day — Billy the Kid.

Before I took my leave from that interesting meeting with the Governor and his wife, Mrs. Wallace took me aside and told me that Governor Wallace was in the midst of writing a novel that she felt had great merit. She said it was a book he had been interested in writing for many years but had never found the time to start. It now appeared he would finally complete it as he had already written several chapters and had even roughed out some drawings that would be used to illustrate the book. She asked me to encourage him to continue with it, which I did. I am happy to report he finished the novel and it turned out to be quite popular. Perhaps you have heard of it. Its title is *Ben Hur*.

Another memorable meeting with another fabulous character from the American West. But the thing that impressed me the most about Governor and Mrs. Wallace was their enduring love for each other.

17

A Little Town in Texas

I have been honored by having many little girls named after me, but when I heard what had happened in Texas it was a tribute beyond belief.

I regret never having met Judge Roy Bean in person because it was through his kindness and devotion that a town in the Southern part of the great state of Texas has been named after me. Timing is such an unpredictable thing in life and it was bad timing on my part that I missed meeting the judge before he passed on.

Let me explain. During my second year in the States, I received an invitation from Judge Bean to visit him in Texas, where he had named a town in my honor. Imagine! A town called Langtry. The judge informed me by letter that he had become a great fan of mine after having seen me perform, I presume in one of the many Texas cities we played. He wrote that he had a large collection of my pictures, posters and newspaper clippings. He soon thereafter got the idea to change the name of the town of Vinegaroon to Langtry. (Being a judge I suppose he had the wherewithal to do so.) While I have had admirers who have collected possibly as much memorabilia as did the judge, never have I had the honor which the judge bestowed upon me by naming a town in my name.

Unfortunately, commitments and contracts prohibited my visiting Langtry, Texas, when I first received Judge Bean's kind invitation. In sending my profound regrets I offered to present an ornamental drinking fountain to the city as a sop; but Roy Bean's quick reply was that it would be quite useless, as the only thing the citizens of Langtry did *not* drink was water! I trust the judge was jesting with me although I must admit, seldom did I see Western men drinking anything as bland as water other than when they were using it to chase the taste away of a stronger beverage they had previously imbibed.

Thus, my chance to visit Langtry and meet my biggest admirer was lost and, regrettably, I was never able to thank him in person for the singular honor he has given me and the Langtry family name.

In trying to learn something of my benefactor I discovered the judge lived quite a flamboyant life. As best I could find out he was born in Kentucky in about 1825. Before he settled in Texas his travels took him to Mexico, then to San Diego, California, and North to Los Angeles, where it is said he killed a man in a dispute over a woman. The story has it that the lady saved Bean's life by cutting the hangman's rope after he had been strung up by the dead man's friends. How true this story is I have no way of knowing.

He was a Southern sympathizer during the Civil War, which found him in New Mexico championing the Confederate cause. Thence on to Texas, where he tried to run the Northern blockade by hauling goods from Mexico. He was married in Texas and sired four children, but his wife eventually took the youngsters and left him, never to return.

Bean, now nearly sixty, was appointed Justice of the Peace in Vinegaroon in 1882 (the year I first arrived in the U.S.) and began his career as the "Law West of the Pecos." Soon thereafter he founded the town of Langtry.

Some years later, I learned Langtry had grown to such an extent that the Southern Pacific Railroad Company had deemed it advisable to establish a station there. In the meanwhile, I received another invitation to visit my name-sake, this time from the "bigwigs" of the township. I decided not to pass up this second opportunity and con-vinced the railway officials to divert our train so we could travel through Texas and on to Langtry. Thankfully, the Southern Pacific officials were willing and I must admit not only was I excitedly looking forward to the visit, but my entire company was thrilled to be a part of our first visit to *my* town.

As we crossed the Pecos River I fervently hoped Judge Bean was looking down from his spot in the heavens with some satisfaction as we moved closer and closer to Langtry.

The weather was characteristically blazing hot as we crossed the Texas desert with its monotonous clothing of sage-brush and low-growing cactus. Suddenly, the Sunset Express came to a sudden stop and as I gazed from the window of the Lalee I saw nothing else but an endless vista of barren desert. I took immediate leave of my private quarters to seek out a staff member so as to inquire whether the train was suffering some sort of malfunction. It had happened before, so it would not have come as a great surprise. However, before I could utter a word, many of my devoted staff made a simultaneous appearance, all an-nouncing in an excited chorus that we had arrived at Langtry!

I am not sure what I was expecting — certainly not a city in the grand manner of London, nor one the likes of San Francisco or even the quaint *pueblo* of Los Angeles. But we had arrived at Langtry, yet there was no habitation in sight. I was then informed that because my private car, the Lalee, was in its usual position at the tail end of the long train, we had not yet come to the city limits. Langtry, was, after all, a "growing" city which had not yet reached quite this far into the Texas desert.

I now refer to my exact notes written immediately after the train pulled away from Langtry to re-live that memorable occasion:

I hurriedly alighted, just as a cloud of sand heralded the approach of a large throng of citizens making their way along the entire length of the train to give me the "glad hand." That the order of the procedure had been thought out and organized was soon evident, for at the head of the ceremonious procession were the officials of the little Texas town, who received me quite heartily.

Justice of the Peace Dodd, a quiet, interesting man, introduced himself, and then presented Postmaster Fielding, Stationmaster Smith, and other persons of consequence. Next in order came a number of cowboys, who were also formally introduced. Langtry did not boast a newspaper, and therefore these young men had been gathered in from the ranges by means of mounted messengers. They were all garbed in their finest leathers and most flamboyant shirts, as became the occasion, making a picturesque group, one loosing off his gun as he passed me, in tangible proof of his appreciation of my visit.

Thirty or forty girls, all about fifteen or sixteen, followed, and were announced *en bloc* as "the young ladies of Langtry." And, finally, "our wives" brought up the rear.

Justice Dodd then welcomed me in an appropriate speech, and, after recounting the history of the town from its inception, declared it would have been the proudest day in the late "King" Bean's life (he had been dead only a few months) if he had lived to meet me, adding with obvious embarrassment, that the judge's eldest son, aged twenty-one, who had been cast for the leading role in this unique reception, had received a sudden summons to San Francisco on important business. But it was generally whispered that he had taken fright at the prospect of the responsible part he was to play, and was lying in hiding somewhere among the universal sagebrush.

The special concession allowed by the railway authorities being limited to half an hour, I was regretfully unable to see the town proper, which lay across the line and some little distance from the tiny wooden shed with "Langtry" written large upon it, and which did duty for the station, but happily the Jersey Lily Saloon was near at hand, and we trudged to it through sagebrush and prickly cactus.

I found it a roughly built wooden two-story house, its entire front being shaded by a piazza, on which a chained monkey gambolled, the latter (installed when the saloon was built) bearing the name of "The Lily" in my honor. The interior of the "Ritz" of Langtry consisted of a long, narrow room, which comprised the entire ground floor, whence a ladder staircase led to a sleeping loft. One side of the room was given up to a bar, naturally the most important feature of the place — while stoutly made tables and a few benches occupied the vacant space. The tables showed plainly that they had been severely used, for they were slashed with Bowie knives, and on each was a well-thumbed deck of playing cards. It was here that Roy Bean, Justice of the Peace, and self-styled "Law West of the Pecos River," used to hold his court and administer justice, which, incidentally, sometimes brought "grist to the mill." The stories I was told of his ready wit and audacity made me indeed sorry that he had not lived long enough to be on hand for my visit.

A tale was related of a Langtryite who had killed a Chinese in a brawl in a neighboring town, where a large number of the so-called "yellow peril" were employed on some special work, the result being that a deputation of the inhabitants arrived at Langtry crying out for vengeance. Roy Bean received his angry visitors in conciliatory spirit, did a thriving business at the bar of the "hotel," housed them in the loft for the night, and left promising to consult his book of law. Returning the next morning the J.O.P. took his accustomed seat on the bar counter with much dignity, and made a speech, discharging the prisoner for the reason that, though he found there was certainly a penalty for killing a white man and a modified penalty for killing a black one, he regretted to say, there was not even an allusion to a yellow one in his famous volume.

This resourceful individual also prospered on a system all his own, which allowed for an immediate divorce and remarriage, until his methods were frowned on by the Government. A story I recall of his ready jurisdiction was that, on being informed that a traveller was lying dead nearby, he went to inspect the corpse. One of the pockets of the dead man sheltered a revolver, and the other contained forty dollars. He judged this case instantly by fining the corpse forty dollars for illegally carrying a revolver and transferring both weapon and money to the commonwealth of Langtry.

We still had a few minutes to see the schoolhouse, which was adjacent to the saloon, but the schoolmistress had sensibly locked the door on this great holiday, so, after

158

pledging myself to send a supply of suitable books from San Francisco, I returned to the train. The cemetery was pointed out to me in the distance, and I was duly informed that only fifteen of the citizens buried there had died natural deaths.

One of the officials, a large, red-bearded, exuberant person, confided to a lady of my company that he deplored not having brought me a keg of fresh-made butter, also that he had a great mind to kiss me, only he didn't know how I would take it, and I thankfully add that Miss Leila Repton had the presence of mind to put a damper on his bold design.

On nearing the train, which was becoming rather impatient, I saw the strange sight of a huge cinnamon bear crossing the line, dragging a cowboy at the end of a long chain. The Lalee was decorated with a good many cages, for on my journey through the South I had acquired a jumping frog at Charleston, an alligator in Florida, a number of horned toads, and a delightfully tame prairie dog called Bob. Hence, I suppose, the correct inference was drawn that I was fond of animals, and the boys resolved to add the late Roy Bean's pet to my collection. They hoisted the unwilling animal on to the platform, and tethered him to the rail, but happily, before I had time to rid myself of this unwelcome addition without seeming discourteous, he broke away, scattering the crowd and causing some of the *vaqueros* to start shooting wildly at all angles.

It was a short visit, but an unforgettable one. As a substitute for the runaway bear, I was presented later with Roy Bean's revolver, which hangs in a place of honor in my English home, and bears the following inscription:

"Presented by W. D. Dodd of Langtry, Texas, to Mrs. Lillie Langtry in honor of her visit to our town. This pistol was formerly the property of Judge Roy Bean. It aided him in finding some of his famous decisions and keeping order West of the Pecos River. It also kept order in the Jersey Lily Saloon. Kindly accept this as a small token of our regards."

I often wonder if Langtry, as the years pass, will grow into one of the major cities in that large and interesting state of Texas.

18

Modjeska the Magnificent

Courage is not the realm of men only. We women also play bravely with the spirit of boldness.

I have worked with many men and women in America, but few have demonstrated as much courage and talent as my dear friend, Helen Modjeska.

I am saddened now to write however, that Helen is no longer with us. She passed away recently. Fortunately, I was able to visit with her just a few weeks before her death.

It was during one of my extended trips through the American West, that I visited this incredibly talented and brave woman, who lay desperately at death's door, suffering from — I was told by her doctor, a young medic from Los Angeles named Dr. Robert Griffith — Bright's disease.

This queen of the stage arts came to America from her native Cracow, Poland, five years before I, in 1877. She arrived with the name Helena Modrzejewski, and soon thereafter conquered America in a manner which I have always envied. Yes, I have always admired and envied two of my closest friends — Helen Modjeska and Sarah Bernhardt.

I have never confessed this before, but never did I possess enough ability to be as eminent an actress as Sarah and Helen.

Of the two however, it has been the talent of Helen Modjeska that I have aspired to. She was Great! Extraordinary! Magnificent! I cannot do her justice with just these written adjectives. When I speak of her, I have been told that my emotions rise to a level that surprises many who do not know me.

I miss Helen, but I am happy I was able to visit with her one last time. After appearing in San Diego I traveled North to Los Angeles with a planned one-day stop at the beautiful beach resort of Newport. If you ever have the chance to visit the Pacific Ocean, do it in Southern California, where the beaches are clean and warm and wonderfully free of clutter and people, and the sunsets wash the sky with painted clouds that will astonish you with overwhelming radiance.

During that stopover, I met with Helen in her Newport Beach home (she had just moved there from her farm in the Santa Ana Mountains near the hamlet of Anaheim, California). It is peculiar, but even though we spend many days and hours with our closest friends, we often know very little of their past life. During this visit, Helen told me much of her life's story, and I believe I was extremely privileged to hear it from her lips, since, as with my own career and life, those who write about us in the press often create a life that indeed we have not endured.

What surprised me the most to learn was that Helen did not come to America to act in plays. She came here to farm.

"I was completely exhausted from my acting work in Poland. My friends and my family talked me into coming to America, where, they said, I could rebuild my strength.

I have always liked farming, wanted to be a farmer, so I bought a little place in El Campo Aleman. That was a German community — now called Anaheim."

I had heard a different story, so I asked. She was honest.

"Oh yes," she said. "I had married Count Bozenta," she smiled at him, he was there next to me, "and he had gotten involved in politics. Unpopular politics. I was indeed exhausted from acting so much."

"They said she was losing her good looks," Count Bozenta said, "that she was fading."

"And he was worried."

"Yes, of course. That and the Russians."

"The Russians?" I asked.

"Yes. I backed a nationalist newspaper and the Russians did not like that."

"So, Lillie, dear friend, we came to America to get away from the Russians, *and my exhaustion.*" She smiled, the victor with the last word — befitting to her reputation.

She then told me that she had brought their son Rudolph and others with her and formed an artists community at her farm. One of these included a recent Nobel prize winner, Henry K. Seinkiewicz, the man who wrote *Quo Vadis* and *Knights of the Cross.*

"We were a happy group in the beginning," she said, "but not for long. I proved to be a total failure at farming."

After that, Count Bozenta suffered many angry rages, mostly out of jealousy. He took his anger out on Henry Seinkiewicz, which soon drove him back to Poland where he wrote his famous works.

And Helen went back to the stage.

"Mostly I returned to acting because California accepted me with open arms," she explained.

I smiled, because I had remembered reports of her first incident with her return. But, before I could say anything, she related the story herself.

"My accent got in my way in San Francisco. It was humiliating. But the manager of the theater — the California — saw in me what he called 'a greatness.'"

I learned that his name was John McCullough. Had it not been for his foresight, we would most likely never have heard of Helen Modjeska.

"He is the one who changed my name from Helena Modrzejewski to what it is," she said laughing lightly, painfully.

"But what did you do with the accent?" I asked.

She smiled and said, "I spoke in my native tongue instead."

After that, she became a major hit.

"What was your favorite play?" I asked.

"Ah," she said. "I followed the great Sarah Bernhardt's lead. I loved Alexander Dumas' *Camille*. And like Sarah, I was always enthusiastic about *Adrienne Lecouvreur*."

"Sarah wrote a great deal of *Camille*."

"Which is why it is so good, no?"

"I am a close friend of Sarah's, as I am with you. I have seen Sarah in each and all of her plays. I have seen you in most of yours. I am telling you now, that in *Camille*, you were vivid, legendary. Much, much better than Sarah," I said. She was gracious when I so complimented her.

"Oh, go away," she said. "Sarah was indeed divine. I have only been called a queen, and you and I each know what queens can be like."

It was my turn to laugh. "Yes, yes," I said. "And the best that I can do is be called a superstar by a judge in Langtry, Texas."

"As long as they believe you are great, then you are great."

"I saw you play Shakespeare at the Court Theater in London. I do believe no woman has ever played Shakespeare better."

"If you keep this up, Lillie, I will have Bozenta throw you out," she chided.

I do believe there were tears welling in her eyes. I nodded that I would refrain from the praise, as most assuredly I could relate.

"I returned to this country after that tour," she volunteered. "I then found myself doing much of what you have done. Travel to nearly every town in America."

"I have enjoyed every day of it."

"And I. I especially have enjoyed working with the likes of Maurice Barrymore and Otis Skinner." She permitted herself to laugh once again — a laugh that was by now very famous.

"I have heard stories about myself that I find humorous," I said. "Are there any you find the same?"

"Oh," she said, her witty charm bubbling to the surface. "At a big dinner party once. It is said that I was asked to recite a play or a piece of one in Polish."

"And?"

"Well, it is told that I put the guests into a fine hypnotic state, that I played all the ranges of emotion — a fine compliment would you not say?"

"I would."

"Well, when I was done with it, someone asked me the name of the play," she laughed with the famous Modjeska lilt and then, catching her breath said, "I told them I had just recited the Polish alphabet."

THE DIARY OF LILLIE LANGTRY

"And the cigarette smoking?" I asked. "You dared to do it in public?"

"Why Lillie, it was because you led the way." She smiled deviously, "Do you happen to have one on you now?"

Count Bozenta stood then, his feathers a bit ruffled. "No! I shall not permit it. You are ill and I intend to get you back to good health."

I nodded agreement. "Maybe next time," I said, taking my cue from the Count and standing alongside him. "I have enjoyed this immensely," I said, leaning down and giving Helen a kiss on her cheek.

"And I," she said weakly, falling back into her pillow. "And I."

I left her then, feeling a heavy weight resting upon my shoulders. This woman who had taken America by storm from New York to California was to leave us at too early an age.

"I will take her back to Cracow," Count Bozenta said as he escorted me to the door.

"There is no hope?"

He only shook his head sadly, and bidding me farewell, he closed the door to their house, producing a soft banging report that seemed too, too final.

My one consolation in thinking of Helen Modjeska is that she will be forever remembered as one of the greatest actresses to grace the American stage. A tribute well deserved.

19

Exceptions to the Rule

I'm amazed at the incredible changes I've seen in America since my first trip here. If growth in the broadest sense of the word indicates success, America's success is assured.

When I first arrived in America, I quickly realized that the settlers of this country were strong people. But it was when I visited the American West that I learned of the spirit of the pioneers who proved to be full of an initiative that exuded a vigor that would, in my opinion back then, bring about a great nation of free people who fought for every inch of land and every breath of air, so that they could have something they could call their own — a nation that no one else could ever put asunder.

To have immigrated here from the tyranny of other worlds, including from my own homeland and that of others, and then to have created a country so vibrant with unbridled growth is to have grasped life as no others on earth ever have. I pray Americans are always able to continue to do so unimpeded by their own rulers or leaders and by outside forces such as those now fighting so savagely in Europe.

One of the big surprises for me came to light recently. When I first came to America, in 1882, women were not looked upon as much more than being responsible for taking care of a husband's household and the family they generated. Women who did not have husbands or who lost their husbands often suffered greatly in America's male-dominated society because women were not permitted to work at regular jobs. This, of course, was a carry over from the traditions brought to America by its original European settlers. But, to its credit, America is a land of change, old-world traditions notwithstanding.

There are exceptions to every rule, of course, and "Charley" Parkhurst was a prime example. Charley never married, although it is said she secretly gave birth to a child. She kept the secret because she had decided early in life to pretend to be a man — so she could work as a stagecoach driver — which she did for some fifty years. Only when she died did those around her learn that she was not the "whipwhacking," tobacco chewing, fist slugging man they thought she was. You can imagine their shock when they discovered Charley's true gender. But I wonder if they sympathized with what she felt was a necessary lifetime charade in order to be able to work at the "man's" job she had chosen?

Unfortunately, other women were not able to pull off the same deception to avoid the ravages of the men who would otherwise control their lives. Many women had to turn to prostitution to survive. Some of these women, I am positive after hearing their stories, would most likely have been model citizens had their husbands not been shot in some bar fight, killed in a mine or died otherwise.

I have met many of these women in my travels here and heard tell of others, who I have recorded in my diary. Of all the women who became prostitutes however, none seized my attention more than a woman in Murray, Idaho.

Her arrival in America, and the story of her first years here resemble my own beginnings so much I often wonder if possibly I, too, might not have fallen into the same dreary trap that Maggie Hall from Dublin, Ireland, who became known as Molly b'Dam, fell into. I missed meeting Molly b'Dam by one week. When I first visited the Couer d'Alenes, (1888), doing a show in Kellogg, a proud mining town just South of Molly's Murray, Molly had already died of consumption. One man among many citizens, each so generous in their praise of Molly — the man's name was Phil O'Rourke — could not refrain from telling me the complete story of this amazing woman.

She was a beautiful young lady about my height of five-feet, eight inches, with bright blonde hair and big blue eyes (very much like mine, I have been told).

When she arrived in Idaho she was but twenty-four. She met a man named Burdan who fell in love with her. After pursuing her relentlessly, he convinced her to marry him. Burdan, like my own husband, Edward Langtry, was receiving a handsome allowance from his father. But when Burdan's father discovered Molly had been a barmaid, he withdrew Burdan's allowance. Edward's father did the same but for different reasons. They had to move out of their quarters to a lesser place. We did, too. Burdan did not cease his gambling after the loss of his allowance and eventually they were near poverty. Poor Edward ran out of money, too, but for other reasons.

Burdan then proved what kind of despicable man he was. He asked Molly to sleep with other men — for money. Her own husband asked her to sell her body to other men. My Edward would never ask such a thing — so the comparison thankfully ends there.

Molly was a devout Catholic. She refused Burdan's request. But Burdan begged and begged until a desperate Molly finally gave in.

Burdan then began bringing men to Molly. After confessing all this to her priest, she was excommunicated, which caused her to believe her soul had been damned.

There was no turning back for Molly after that. From then on, beginning at the age of twenty-four, Molly lived her life as a sinner. She left Burdan and traveled from mining camp to mining camp — even to San Francisco and Chicago and other well known gambling towns, finally ending up in Deadwood, South Dakota, where she met Calamity Jane and Wild Bill Hickok — all the time selling her body.

During this period, her price rose to great heights. She presented herself in expensive clothes including furs and diamonds. Her success meant nothing to her, however, since, to her way of thinking, she had no soul.

By the time she was thirty, she was fairly well to do and when she read of the gold strike in the Couer d'Alenes, she decided to take her business there. She took a train from Deadwood to Montana and thereafter rode horseback through deep snow to Murray.

She joined a pack train and during the hardest part of the trip, she saved the lives of a mother and her child.

By the time she reached Murray, word had spread of the gorgeous woman who had acted so bravely.

For Molly, Murray became her permanent home. Upon her arrival she was delighted to learn that much of the citizenry was comprised of Irish immigrants. Her first friend in Murray also turned out to be the one who was at her bedside when she died — the man who told me her story, Phil O'Rourke. It was O'Rourke who dubbed her

Molly b'Dam. He told me it was because he misunderstood her when she told him her name was Molly Burdan. Others claim another story which I find specious and not worthy of repeating.

Apparently, Molly announced upon arrival that she would be the town's Madam. She was accepted with open arms and in fact, became the town's Madam.

It is the legend of Molly's activities other than prostitution that attracted my attention, reasons which made her so beloved to her community. I believe that were it not for her husband, Burdan, she might very well have become a great medical nurse.

Two years before I arrived in Kellogg, smallpox visited its ravages upon Murray. The town, not having any leadership, suffered quickly with people hiding in their homes or trying to escape the smallpox by leaving.

As it turned out, it was Molly who "saved the town." She called for a town meeting and announced that only cowards run away. She told them that she had ordered her girls to take care of the people at her end of town and that every healthy person should pitch in to save their friends. According to Mr. O'Rourke, Molly put an energy back into the town and those who could, administered to those who became deathly ill.

"But it was Molly who worked without ending," Mr. O'Rourke told me, "until the town survived."

Unfortunately, her heroics eventually took her own life. But the town did not forget, nor I believe, will they ever.

What has amazed me mostly since my first trip is that today women hold many important jobs in America — along with that of family matriarch.

Today, because of the war raging in Europe, and since President Wilson has finally put America into that war, millions of American women are employed outside their home in jobs traditionally held by men. Women are producing war materiel, working as lorry drivers and even running some railroad yards.

But of all these changes, the one that impresses me the most concerns the woman I met on this, my last journey to New York, where I must catch my ship home.

Jeannette Rankin of Montana, a Republican in this country, a woman not through her thirties, has been elected to represent her state of Montana in the United States Congress. She is the first woman ever to be elected to the U.S. Congress. I believe, after having met her, that she will do a fine job representing her people. I only hope that some day my own Parliament might include women. After all, we have had some rather impressive queens, including my favorite, Victoria.

It is also a change for America to expand its growing burst of industrial power and enter our war in Europe — although I am not surprised. After all, the spirit of which I refer concerning Americans is that they not only fight for what they want and they will quickly defend others who they feel are in trouble. The country has grown strong, healthy and to the amazement of those with whom I have become friendly, sophisticated in international affairs.

The mere fact that the local newspapers have announced that it costs $156 to outfit a doughboy is enough to demonstrate their commitment. That is a lot of money for this country to spend on anyone's war, including their own.

Everywhere I venture these days, there are huge posters — painted by an American artist named James Montgomery Flagg — of Uncle Sam pointing out to the viewer that America "wants you." The country recently passed into law something called the Selective Draft Act.

THE DIARY OF LILLIE LANGTRY

Over 500,000 American men, selected by the American government, are being sent to Europe to fight our war. The excitement of General Pershing — they call him "Black Jack" here — recently landing in Europe has spurred many a young American man to volunteer for the army. I do pray this does not create many young widows, because after the war, I fear there will not be the same jobs available for women that there are now — and I do not wish to see any woman have to resort to selling her body to men in order to survive. There should not have to be any more Molly b'Dam stories.

However, there is a small group of women here who now call themselves suffragists. These feminists, two vociferous ladies, Jane Addams and Carrie Chapman Catt among them, do not want women in the war effort. Another cause for concern is that labor unions here do not permit women to join their ranks. Consequently the health and pay of working women goes neglected. Public speculation about what will happen to these women when the war is over is made in the newspapers every day and I must say, what I read is not at all the America I believe I have come to know. The articles that irritate me the most are the ones wherein the editors write that it will be the "patriotic duty of these women to leave their pursuits as soon as the men return from the war."

I truly believe there is a new era dawning for women not only in America but throughout the world. We will soon be taking our rightful position of equals to men, a role I think long overdue.

20

Pathfinder, Politician, Pauper

The note I received backstage was cryptic: "Could you leave tickets for someone who will never again have a chance to see you?" Of course, I did.

I first met General John C. Fremont and his beautiful and charming wife, Jessie, while near the end of my first cross-country tour of the United States. It was 1883 and he was governor of the Arizona Territory. He and Mrs. Fremont had attended our performance of *She Stoops to Conquer* in the territorial capital of Prescott and were gracious enough to make it a point to introduce themselves to me. At the time I did not realize what an important figure in the history of America General Fremont was.

Some time later I met a man named Ned Buntline, who said he was a writer who specialized in stories of the West, and who had been in the theater the night I performed for the Fremonts. He asked me if I knew much about them. I confessed to him that I did not and he proceeded to tell me the story of this most interesting husband and wife.

John Charles Fremont was born in Savannah, Georgia, in 1813. He was the illegitimate son of a Frenchman named Jean Charles Fremon and eventually Anglicized his last name by adding a "t" at the end. He was educated at the College of Charleston as a civil engineer and began his professional career as a railway surveyor. In 1838 he was commissioned a second lieutenant in the U.S. Corps of Topographical Engineers, an elite group of about thirty-five men whose mission it was to chart maps for the ever expanding United States of America. With this appointment he began a short but brilliant tenure as an explorer of the American West and, as so often is the case, probably spent the happiest days of his life in carrying out this assignment although there were many greater and more important events lying ahead of him.

In 1842 he was assigned to explore the road to Oregon as far as the Wind River mountains in Western Wyoming. These were the days when the pioneers were heading West in greater numbers than ever before, yet trails were few and far between. Fremont was highly successful in his efforts and the U.S. government then placed him in charge of an expedition to the Pacific Coast the following year. His journeys took him to Fort Vancouver, then across the Sierra Nevada through unchartered territory, to Fort Sutter in California and into what was then Mexican territory, thence back over the Rocky Mountains to Missouri.

By 1845 there was considerable interest in the United States in acquiring California and other adjacent territories which were controlled by the Mexicans. Fremont was sent on another expedition to California, eventually raising the U.S. flag in the Gabilan Mountains before prudently withdrawing North to Oregon rather than face an over-whelming contingent of irate Mexican militiamen. When the Mexican War broke out he was appointed commandant and governor of California by Commodore Robert Stockton, but a disagreement between Fremont and General Stephen Kearny, who succeeded Stockton, led to Fremont's court martial and a sentence of dismissal from the army.

President James Knox Polk canceled the punishment but Fremont resigned his commission as lieutenant colonel and thereafter served from 1850 to 1851 as U.S. senator from California.

Fremont met his future wife, Jessie, in 1841 and they were secretly married later that year despite the fact she was only seventeen years old. Jessie's father was Senator Thomas Hart Benton, a senator from Missouri and self-proclaimed father of Manifest Destiny. Let me explain what that was, as best I can recall from what Ned Buntline told me: The doctrine that came to be called Manifest Destiny had its beginnings in the 1830s. It put forth the theory that God had created a new breed of man, mainly of English and Scottish heritage, Protestant in religion, democratic in ideology, and white in color, that was destined to rule North America from the Atlantic to the Pacific, and from the Canadian border in the North to the Gulf of Mexico and California to the South. The only problem at the time was there were several other nations laying claim to territories that the believers in Manifest Destiny said rightfully belonged to the Americans: England claimed what was called the Oregon Territory, all land North of California; Mexico ruled over California and Texas and much of the land in the Southwest. Indeed, even the Russians had moved down the West Coast but seemed more content to reign over Alaska.

The American citizens who were believers in Manifest Destiny — and they numbered in the millions — did not claim the disputed land was theirs by right of discovery or even settlement. Rather, they maintained, it was an act of Providence which gave them the right to the land. Thus the complicated issue evolved, eventually being settled pretty much as the espousers of Manifest Destiny demanded, but not without bloodshed as climaxed by the American war with Mexico.

No one could have been better cast to enter into this fray than John Charles Fremont. And he could not have had a closer connection to the battle than to fall in love and marry the daughter of the prime mover of Manifest Destiny. But Senator Benton was totally opposed to Jessie, his favorite child, marrying John. So much that when he heard of their secret marriage he exploded at Fremont, "Get out of my house and never cross my door again! Jessie shall stay here."

But Jessie stood by her new husband not only at the outset of their marriage but for the rest of her days with him. She told him, "Whither thou goest, I will go; and where thou lodgest, I will lodge."

Senator Benton, no doubt realizing that nothing would change his strong-willed daughter's love for Fremont, soon relented and not only forgave his son-in-law, but became one of his strongest supporters. It was, in fact, Senator Benton who got Fremont the assignment to map the Oregon Trail in 1842.

It was while on this first expedition that Fremont hired as a guide a man who was destined to become an American legend — Kit Carson. Born in 1809 in Kentucky, Carson was uneducated and illiterate. But what he lacked in education he more than made up for by his knowledge of scouting and mountaineering. He was strong and level headed, quite a contrast to the impulsive Fremont. And, despite having no schooling, Carson could get along quite well in French, Spanish and several Indian dialects.

The two made an interesting team and, in fact, joined together for three expeditions. A fourth expedition which Fremont undertook without Carson's assistance as a guide nearly proved fatal for Fremont when he became snowed in and almost died. He was able to make his way to Taos, New Mexico, however, and recuperated at Carson's house.

Carson, who had settled permanently in Taos, served as an army scout during the Mexican War, then became an Indian agent, and during the Civil War he achieved the rank of general in the Union army and spent his time in the Southwest campaigning against hostile Indian tribes. He returned to his farm in Taos after the war and died following a hunting accident in 1868.

Fremont, meanwhile, had an unexpected turn of good luck. Land he had obtained in California turned out to have gold on it and he became a rich man.

His short tenure as a U.S. Senator and his other exploits gained him enough national attention to warrant his nomination as the first Republican candidate for president. While he did well and carried all but five Northern states, he was defeated by his rival, Democrat James Buchanan.

During the Civil War Fremont served as a major general and commander of the Department of the West. He was a favorite of the Radical Republicans, who favored immediate emancipation and harsh measures against the South. He even went so far as to issue a military emancipation proclamation in Missouri, thus arousing the ire of the border states. President Lincoln, uncomfortable with the peripatetic Fremont, soon thereafter removed him from his command of the Department of the West. In 1864 Fremont was nominated to run for president by the Radical Republicans who were attempting to thwart Lincoln's re-election, but he withdrew from the race after an agreement between his and Lincoln's supporters.

Fremont's fortunes began to decline after the war and it was Jessie's voluminous writings that helped support the family. His speculations in the railroad business ended in failure and his star shone brightly for one last time between 1878 and 1883 when he was governor of the Arizona Territory.

I have since learned that the general died poverty stricken on July 13, 1890, in New York City — not long after his request to come see my play. Sadly, an act of Congress to restore him to the rank of retired major general with a full pension came too late to do him any good.

Ironically, it is Fremont — not more famous Americans like Washington, Lincoln, Jefferson and the like — who has more geographical areas in Western America named after him than any other man. In fact, I have traveled through Fremont, Ohio, Fremont, Nebraska and Fremont, California, just three of the many areas named in his honor.

After Ned Buntline finished his story of General Fremont I found myself intrigued not by what he had told me about Mrs. Fremont, but what he had *not* told me. During our brief meeting I sensed that here was a uniquely strong woman who was totally devoted to her husband. I asked Mr. Buntline if my feelings had any validity and he was quick to give me credit for an astute observation.

"Jessie Fremont is as ambitious a woman as I have ever known," Mr. Buntline told me. "And I don't say this in any derogatory manner," he quickly added. "Her ambition — her passion — always was her husband and the acknowledgment of his achievements she felt was never truly given him."

"But the man was a general, a U.S. senator, presidential candidate...certainly that was acknowledgement of his greatness," I said.

"To a degree, yes. But he seemed to overshadow every achievement with failure," Mr. Buntline maintained. "In fact, if it wasn't for Jessie he wouldn't have what recognition he has today."

He went on to tell me that not only he, but many people begrudgingly felt that Jessie was truly the power behind the throne when it came to General Fremont. She was constantly at his side as an advisor, chief aide and supporter.

"Some people called her 'General Jessie,'" Mr. Buntline said. "In fact old Abe Lincoln said she was a 'female politician,' and I don't think he was trying to be kind. But Jessie got back at him. She called Lincoln 'an ass' — in private, mind you. She was too much a lady to say it in public."

Jessie Fremont was not a lady who was intimidated by Washington, D.C. — remember, her father was a prominent senator, so she spent many days in the nation's capital. She was not above lobbying for her husband's causes no matter what government big wig she had to try to influence.

In 1856, when General Fremont was nominated for president, she stood by him throughout until critics began to call it the "Fremont and Jessie" campaign. In fact, Jessie was so prominent a personality that women suffragist's hopes to get the vote suddenly took a decided upswing.

Unfortunately, for all the exciting times that Jessie and the general spent together, there was just as much if not more time spent apart. He was constantly on the go — whether it was as an officer during the war or a businessman involved in one of his many railroad promotions. Jessie would join him when she could, oftentimes against great odds. On one occasion, when the general was in California during the gold rush, Jessie, with their six-year-old daughter, crossed the Isthmus of Panama by dugout and mule to get to her husband. She was a devoted and intensely loyal wife and many friends referred to General Fremont as "Jessie's insanity."

When General Fremont's career reached its nadir, it was Jessie's writings that supported the family. In fact, it is she who is credited with making Kit Carson an American legend, and it is through her inspired writings that history will remember the many achievements of her illustrious husband.

Although I never saw the Fremonts again on my subsequent trips to America, I did learn that after the general's death Jessie took up residence in Los Angeles, where she continues with her writing. I wish her well.

I was pleased to leave the tickets to our play in New York. They were, as you have surmised, for John and Jessie Fremont, but, unlike our first visit, they did not come backstage this time. I wish they had.

21

The Notorius Doctor

Why is it that, so often, men actually believe they are more capable than women of equal ability?

I first met Mary Walker while in New York. She caught my attention when the New York *Morning Telegraph* second-page story headlined her as a "notorious" doctor from the Civil War who had been arrested in the city for "causing a disturbance" in front of Macy's when other shoppers swarmed about her. Apparently, the store manager called the police to protect her, but instead she got into an argument with them. The paper then went on to say she had spent the previous three months involved in charges and counter charges, a few court hearings and the brunt of many editorial cartoons.

But in the photographs published in the papers I noticed the American Congressional Medal of Honor pinned to the lapel of her coat. (She wore men's clothes all the time for a very sound reason: her symbol of equality to men and her defiance to the regimen that women could not wear male styled clothes). I knew from her pictures that I would like her.

And indeed I did when I met her. She has a history that I envy. She is a fighter, a woman with many causes, but each supporting women's rights.

She has fought for the right of women to vote in the United States. She believed strongly the U.S. Constitution already gave women that right. And she has fought for the right of women to wear comfortable clothing.

Mary Walker spoke before Congress concerning the women's right to vote. "As long as you tax women and deprive them of the right of franchise, you but make yourselves tyrants," she argued. "I am opposed to granting men the right to vote on the rights of women," she declared.

But to no avail.

To better understand Mary Walker, I visited her again when next in New York City and we had an extraordinary discussion during dinner.

"When the Civil War broke out," she told me, "I was 29. I had just been divorced and was anxious to help my country. I was a doctor, having graduated from Syracuse Medical College in upstate New York, and so went to Washington to seek a commission in the army as a medical officer."

I asked her if it was common for the army to have women doctors. She laughed lightly and said, "No, not then, not now."

She went on to explain they assigned her to the U.S. Patent Office which had been turned into a temporary hospital, but only as an administrator.

"Women cannot be doctors of men," they told me. "A woman can be nothing more than a mother or housewife," was the official position.

But I already knew she had served as a doctor with the Union army, so naturally, I asked, "But how did you finally end up at the Battle of Bull Run?"

Mary Walker was cordial in her response. "I crossed into Virginia, into enemy territory, to meet with General Ambrose E. Burnside," she said.

"The man who commanded the entire Union army?"

She nodded. "Yes. When I got there, I found the most vile of conditions in the field hospitals. Medical staffs were too exhausted to do anyone any good. The medical equipment was thoroughly inadequate. When I pointed all this out to the General, he approved my moving the patients from the battlefield to Washington. I helped transport them North. That was the beginning of a long arduous course to get the army's approval. Women volunteers met the train with food and drink, but even they would not serve any of the nourishment to me."

"But why?"

"I was wearing pants and a straw hat with an ostrich feather stuck in it. They must have found me, well, not one of them."

When I sat back, appearing completely chagrined, she added, "Even President Abraham Lincoln would have nothing to do with me. When I wrote to President Lincoln, requesting a commission, he returned my note with this handwritten message." She handed me a note with Lincoln's message scrawled across the bottom. "I cannot fulfill your request to obtain a commission. If the medical director of the army wishes to appoint you, I am willing, but I am sure controversy on the subject will not subserve the public interest."

"What did you do after this?" I asked, handing the note back to her.

"I went back to the battlefield where I learned that a surgeon in the Ohio regiment had been killed in Tennessee. I stepped in, on a temporary basis mind you, to take his place."

"And it went smoothly after that?"

"Hardly. When the medical director of the Cumberland army discovered my presence, he called me a 'medical monstrosity' and ordered a review of my skills. He appointed an examining board and of course they informed him I was incompetent — that my medical knowledge was that of a housewife." She sighed and added, "Of course I was not incompetent. As a matter of fact I found my skills either on a par with the best of their doctors, sometimes much better."

"But your Medal of Honor?"

"Bull Run is what President Johnson's citation reads, but I tell everyone that the special valor was for going into the enemy's ground, when the inhabitants were suffering from professional service, and sent to our lines to beg assistance; and no man surgeon was willing to respond for fear of being taken prisoner; and by doing so the people were won over to the Union." She smiled when she said this, then added, "The army hates that response."

"I read in the *Telegraph* that you were taken prisoner."

"Yes. I was sent to Richmond Prison, which was also known as Castle Thunder. It was a covered tobacco warehouse. After a few months I was exchanged for a Confederate major. That's when the army finally figured out that a woman could do some of the things a man can do. They awarded me a contract as an acting assistant surgeon when I returned."

"And the commission?"

"No. Never. Andrew Johnson even notes that in my citation."

The following is a copy of the citation and declaration of battle issued to Mary Walker, signed by President Andrew Johnson. Note the many references to "contract" and "civilian." Also, in 1917, the Board of Medal Awards (created by the Act of 3 June 1916), after reviewing the merits of the awardees of the Civil War awards, ruled Dr. Walker's medal, as well as those of 910 other recipients as unwarranted. Dr. Walker's was clearly retracted because of her gender).

Rank and organization: Contract Acting Assistant Surgeon (civilian), U.S. Army. Places and dates: Battle of Bull Run, July 21, 1861; Patent Office Hospital, Washington, D.C., October 1861; Chattanooga, Tenn., following Battle of Chickomauga, September 1863; Prisoner of War, April 10, 1864-August 12, 1864, Richmond Va.; Battle of Atlanta, September 1864. Entered service at: Louisville, Ky. Born: 26 November 1832, Oswego County, N.Y.

Whereas it appears from official reports that Dr. Mary E. Walker, a graduate of medicine, "has rendered valuable service to the Government, and her efforts have been earnest and untiring in a variety of ways," and that she was assigned to duty and served as an assistant surgeon in charge of female prisoners at Louisville, Ky., upon the recommendations of Major-Generals Sherman and Thomas, and faithfully served as contract surgeon in the service of the United States, and has devoted herself with much patriotic zeal to the sick and wounded soldiers, both in the field and hospitals, to the detriment of her own health, and has also endured hardships as a prisoner of war four months in a Southern prison while acting as contract surgeon; and

Whereas by reason of her not being a commissioned officer in the military service, a brevet or honorary rank cannot, under existing laws, be conferred upon her; and

Whereas in the opinion of the President an honorable recognition of her services and sufferings should me made:

It is ordered, That a testimonial thereof shall be hereby made and given to the said Dr. Mary E. Walker, and that the usual Medal of Honor for meritorious services be given her.

Given under my hand in the city of Washington, D.C., this 11th day of November, A.D. 1865.

Andrew Johnson,
President
By the President:
Edwin M. Stanton
Secretary of War

I have observed in my total of twenty years in America that the Civil War years were an introduction to a half-century of women aspiring to many lost causes — most of which I have fully supported. Mary Walker was just another drum beater for the rights of women. Fortunately for women, she was an important drum beater because she helped open the door to women who want to become doctors, women who may wish to serve their country in the military and she definitely opened the debate for women's rights in wearing whichever kind of clothes they wish to wear.

Her relentless campaign to obtain voting rights for women has been overwhelmed in the press by the defense of her Congressional Medal of Honor which was taken away from her by an act of Congress — simply because she was a woman.

While I have often praised the Americans for their forward thinking as compared to the rest of the world, let it never be forgotten that the battle for equal rights for women has certainly not been won. There are thousands of unsung women in American history who, when the day of total equality comes, will long be forgotten. However, that does not mean they did not make a contribution, no matter how large or small, to the forward march of women. I have been fortunate because of the acceptance by both men and women of whatever talents I may possess as an actress, to be allowed to dabble in a realm once restricted to men — such as the ownership of my own touring company and theater, for example. But even I have had to tread lightly at times, such as not calling my racing stable by my own name but as owned by "Mr. Jersey." Women, I feel, are blessed by having a great deal of patience — but our day will come.

Women in America will soon get the vote, of that I am convinced — and at that time, Mary Walker's work will not have gone in vain.

22

We Call Her "Granny"

At first I felt like an intruder at this very private family affair, but soon I forgot my place and found myself joining in on the debate.

During my previous extended trip to America, in 1903, I was invited to an American Thanksgiving dinner by a family known to be "high society." I had no idea it would be as delightful and interestingly Americana as it turned out.

Let me interject here that I find the Thanksgiving holiday a wonderful, typically American idea. It comes about a month before Christmas, but gives families a chance to gather without the necessity of gift giving and frantic pace that seems to take over at Christmas. Leave it to the Americans.

My friends, Stanley Mortimer and his wife Tissie, arranged the invitation for this Thanksgiving of 1903. The Mortimers were close friends of Sara, the hostess of the dinner party. Mostly, I was informed by Stanley, "it will be a family affair, with just a few close friends, and you, of course, my dear Lillie."

THE DIARY OF LILLIE LANGTRY

It seems that Sara had seen me in New York playing Rosalind in *As You Like It*, and that she very much liked my performance and wanted to meet me.

I was only too happy to have a place to visit on Thanksgiving. In America, it is one of the largest family reunion days of the year. Whole cities empty while Americans travel *en masse* to their roots as it were, to join for a day of family gathering and feasting. I do not cherish being alone at such times, so naturally I accepted the invitation.

When I arrived, I was met graciously at the door of a great white house in Fairhaven by Warren (the III, I learned later), brother of the hostess. Warren was quite good looking, taller than I, of executive composure with an air of wealth about him.

When Warren opened the door, I quickly caught the aroma of turkeys roasting in the kitchen and the sounds of a large family already gathered, and from the level of chatter I assumed the guests were quite possibly tipping more than one alcoholic beverage. They were gay, happy, certainly a solid family.

"Lillie Langtry," Warren announced to the group after leading me to the large room where they were gathered. They paused, a few raising their glasses to me and said in unison, "Welcome, Lillie Langtry."

For a moment, I was sure they did not know who I was, and I was also positive that Stanley Mortimer had not warned them of my pending arrival. But a young man quickly assuaged those fears, stepping from the crowd of family members which included cousins, godfathers, grandparents, brothers and sisters and came straight to me. "Good afternoon," he said in a distinct, rounded voice. "Please, come in and join us. We have been expecting you."

"Well," I said, without much forethought, "I'm relieved to hear that."

He smiled, then chuckled, then gently taking my arm, escorted me about the room, introducing me to everyone, one at a time, until finally we came to Eleanor. "This is cousin Eleanor," he said. "We call her granny."

Eleanor, standing as erect as any woman I've ever seen or known, smiled briskly and shook my hand. "It's lovely to meet you Mrs. Langtry. I was with Sara when she saw you in New York. You were, well, divine."

I flushed. "Oh, my," I said. "Thank you so very much."

"Sara is dying to meet you. You should find her, well, quite interesting. "My gaze quickly captured an image of Eleanor that remains to this day. She was sweet, although pathetically so, eager to please me with a kindness that showed. She was, as Americans are wont to say, a bit of a wallflower — although I would state it differently by simply saying she is not particularly beautiful. She was not ugly, having large illuminating eyes that were lovely to look at, and she did have a good figure and a fine complexion. Unfortunately her teeth protruded over a slightly receding chin which contributed more to her not being beautiful than anything else. It must have been her own knowledge of all this that seemed to cause an awkwardness that she should not have felt among her own family — but apparently did.

"Come," Stanley Mortimer said to me, pulling me away from Eleanor, "you must meet Sara, your hostess."

Sara was the one woman at the party that the young man had not introduced me to — simply because she was not yet there at that time.

Stanley led me to Sara. One look at Sara and I thought possibly Eleanor's words were a warning rather than a description. Everything about Sara spoke *Matriarch*. She appeared at least a decade younger than her actual age, yet sternly in control of her family; everyone at the dinner was her family, even distant cousins from her husband's family were taken in by her as being her wards. That was the obvious.

What was not obvious to me at first, was an air of tension in the room when I entered. How could it be. Family secrets that are about to burst into the open are not generally known by anyone but those privy to the secrets. And in this case, that included only two people in the room, yet there was a buzz going around, because when family members seem to hold back on something, other family members are able to detect the difference in stature, attitude and probably voice.

"So nice to meet you," Sara said. "I loved you in *As You Like It*."

"Thank you," I said. "And thank you so much for inviting me to your family dinner. New York City can be such a lonely place for outsiders during these holiday times."

"You are not an outsider Lillie," Sara said with the matriarchal tones I expected from her. "You are now family."

I didn't know how to respond to those words, but bowed my head slightly and said simply, "You are too kind."

She accepted my words graciously and then said, "Have you met my son?"

I wasn't sure. "I have met most everyone here," I said, turning back to face the group. "Which is he?"

She pointed out the young man who had come to my rescue earlier. "That one." She motioned the young man over and he came to her like a trained puppy might to his master.

"Yes, mummy," he said.

"I want you to keep Mrs. Langtry here entertained this evening, will you do that?

"He smiled comfortably. "Yes, of course. Mrs. Langtry," he said, placing his arm up for me to grasp, "you shall not be bored."

And I was not!

Moments later he made an announcement that rocked the party so noticeably that some of them found dinner difficult to swallow.

Sara's son and his dear lady friend, Eleanor Roosevelt, niece of the president of the United States, Teddy Roosevelt, and cousin to the young man I came to admire — Franklin Delano Roosevelt, announced to their family and friends, that they would soon "accept the vows of marriage."

Two cousins with the same last name would marry, unless Sara Delano Roosevelt, Franklin's mother, could stop it!

Sara's demeanor changed with that announcement. She visibly staggered. "I cannot believe this, Franklin," she shouted. She declared this was a terrible surprise, that Franklin "had never been in any sense a ladies man."

Family members rushed to her side to help her find a chair into which she might sit and catch her breath. I stood by, not knowing where to place myself in the room, for it was a bit exciting, embarrassing and I must admit, titillating in the sense that I had been present for such a surprise announcement. I listened while Sara rambled on, sometime incoherently, other times nonsensically.

"I don't believe I remember ever hearing him talk about girls," she said. Then, "He is still in college. Harvard for heaven's sake. He can't get married."

She carried on like that a while, saying also that Franklin had only recently voted for the first time, that he'd never held a money-paying job — that in essence he was simply too young to get married. Too young to understand what love was.

Her inner feelings about this marriage, however, came forth when she declared, "Why, he has never consulted me about this. He has not asked my advice. And he is going to marry Eleanor Roosevelt! He has not asked my permission!"

Franklin at that point stepped in to the foray and informed his mother, "This is a truly irrevocable fact, Mummy! I am going to be married to Eleanor."

"You cannot!" she declared.

"But I can," he argued plaintively.

"She cannot, she cannot even play sports. She is a poor sailor, you know that. You love to sail."

"She can watch from the shoreline."

"She is only nineteen, Franklin," Sara stated flatly, the strong matriarch returning. "You would be robbing the cradle."

"We will wait until I am through with college. She will be twenty-one then."

And so it went, for another half hour, when finally the butler entered the room of stunned guests and announced dinner. His words fell on deaf ears. He rang the bell and finally getting their attention, he was able to get us into the dining room where we enjoyed a sumptuous meal — somewhat silently.

Two weeks later I was invited to lunch by Stanley Mortimer who said in his written invitation he felt he owed me a "delightful meal" after the incident at Fairhaven. I could not reach him to tell him he did not owe me anything, that

194

I rather found the incident to be entertaining, delightful and nothing more than a son and his mother coming to a meeting of emotions concerning the son's breaking away from his mother's control. So, I met Stanley at a small restaurant (with rather high prices for meals) in Mid-Manhattan Island.

To my delight, he had Sara with him. It was Sara who turned out to beg forgiveness of the Thanksgiving day.

"It was so dreadful of me to come apart thusly," she said. "I had guests to consider and I completely forgot them, especially you. I am so sorry," she said.

"Quite all right," I responded, meaning it. "I had a delightful day."

"Well," she said, "I felt I owed you an apology and an explanation. You see, Franklin is so dear to me that I was hurt when he made that announcement. I had no inkling of his involvement with his cousin. None. I felt that my son had been deliberately secretive, that he had taken great pains to keep his secret from me. That is what caused me to come to pieces. Please believe me when I say it was not Eleanor, nor his liking Eleanor that caused my reaction. We spent last summer together at Hyde Park and I got to know her intimately. She is a dear, sweet girl, certainly one with perfect suitability for Franklin in terms of family and social standing."

She paused, I waited.

"No mother wants to learn that her son has kept secrets from her. It was as though he had cast me aside, that he no longer loved me."

"That possibly, he loved her more?"

She nodded, yes. "I am afraid so."

"Have you changed your mind since then?"

She glanced away, then back to me. She was pulling paper out of her purse when she continued. "I have read all about you Mrs. Langtry."

"Please call me Lillie."

She smiled. "Yes, of course. Lillie. You are a worldly woman. You know more people than any Delano or Roosevelt save possibly for Uncle Teddy — who I have learned — you have met."

"Yes, he gave me a tour of the White House."

"And not me?" We laughed lightly together, then she said, "First let me explain. A week after Thanksgiving, I invited Eleanor to my apartment in New York City. I had a long talk with the dear child. I explained that Franklin had a career to get started, that he had not yet graduated from college nor from law school which he has still to attend. I explained that it was not a good idea for cousins to marry and finally, I may have been too rough, but I told her honestly that I did not wish to see this marriage take place."

"What did she say?"

"Nothing. Until I received a letter from her."

"Oh!" I must have cocked an eye or something because she handed me the letters she held in her hand (from her purse).

"Because you are who you are, and have lived every life I believe possible, I wish to show you these two letters and obtain from you an opinion of what I should do from this point on. I recognize that I am rigid, sometimes unfair. I do not wish this marriage to take place, I fear for my son's career. He is a bright young man who promises to have a great future. I do not wish this girl to ruin all that."

I quickly read the letters.

(From Eleanor)

"Dearest Cousin Sallie,

I must thank you for being so good to me yesterday. I know just how you feel and how hard it must be, but I do so want you to learn to love me a little. You must know that I will always try to do what you wish for I have grown to love you very dearly during the last summer. It is impossible for me to tell you how I feel toward Franklin. I can only say that my one great wish is always to prove worthy of him.

Love,
Eleanor"

(From Franklin)

"Dearest Mama,

I know what pain I must have caused you and you know I wouldn't do it if I really could have helped it — *mais tu sais, me voila!* that's all that could be said — I know my mind, have known it for a long time, and know that I could never think otherwise: Result: I am the happiest man just now in the world; likewise the luckiest. And for you, dear Mummy, you know that nothing can ever change what we have always been and will always be to each other — only now you have two children to love and to love you — and Eleanor as you now will always be a daughter to you in every way.

Love you always,
Franklin"

I handed the letters back to Sara and sighing heavily said, "I believe they love each other, Sara. I do not believe there is much other you can do but approve it and love them with all your heart."

That was not the direction she wanted to hear from me. "Thank you," she said crisply. Then softening a little she added, "I mean it. Thank you. But, I cannot condone this

197

marriage. I must delay it, force more time between now and their planned wedding so that they might get to know each other more and also have the chance to meet others. They are too young to know what they want. Too young to start a family. Such matters bring grave responsibilities."

"Many happy marriages begin at their age."

"My father did not marry until he was thirty-three by which time he was a man who had made a name and a place for himself. He had something to offer a woman."

"And Franklin? What of his emotions? His desires?"

"He has nothing of his own to offer her. His inheritance form his father was small one. He is living off my wealth. Therefore, he must develop his own career to continue living at the standard both he and Eleanor have become accustomed to."

"But he wishes to be a lawyer. Surely he will do well."

"He must spend another four years in college, then law school and then it takes two years to pass the bar examination. It is the better part of wisdom to delay this marriage, to wait. At least until he is a member of a good law firm."

"May I offer some advice?"

Sara glanced about a moment, then with reluctance in her voice, she said, "Yes."

I glanced to Stanley who had been impeccably silent during this discourse, then back to Sara. "You run the risk of alienating Eleanor. Mark my words, Sara, Franklin will marry her. If you interfere too much, they may marry earlier than you wish, and Eleanor and you will end up never speaking to each other — and that could make Franklin's life miserable."

"Nonsense! If I am successful, and I am always successful, the marriage will not occur and it won't matter if Eleanor speaks to me or not."

With that she rose from the table and taking her bow, bid us adieu and departed.

"Well," Stanley said quietly, "that is probably the last I will see of her."

I put my hand on his arm and shook my head. "No, she won't even remember you were here."

"She will do it, you know?"

"What?"

"Try every tactic in the book to stop that marriage."

I nodded agreement but said, "Whatever she tries, it won't work. It will only drive them closer together."

Now, during this trip to America, I have learned the outcome of this encounter. Sara did indeed attempt to drive a wedge between Franklin and Eleanor. Although she caused some minor rifts between the couple, the first when she sent Franklin on a Caribbean cruise in early 1904. Later at Campobello while Franklin courted Eleanor, Sara often attempted to stop the relationship, but by then Eleanor had caught on and nothing Sara could do would stop them.

Eleanor's Auntie Bye, Teddy Roosevelt's sister, insisted that Eleanor come to Washington for the winter of 1904, which she did. While there, she spent a few nights in the White House, where "Uncle Ted" introduced her to a life of supreme power and all the obligations that came with it.

Accompanying her Auntie Bye, she was a guest at daily teas, luncheons, dinners and cocktail parties where she met international diplomats, government officials, politicians and celebrities — people who were performing great and noble duties in the world. Important people. During the course of this, she developed her own "charm and wit and *savior faire.*" She learned to remain at ease at these events, developing a knowledge of her own talents which were a quick witted mind that was capacious and retentive.

She became an intelligent conversationalist, a personality to deal with. She learned, as many of us in public life do, to set off an impression that she was more knowledgeable than she actually was.

In other words, Eleanor Roosevelt blossomed during the Winter of 1904.

The engagement of Franklin to Anna Eleanor Roosevelt was announced in November, 1904 and they were married in March of 1905.

23

Mr. Masterson, I Presume

I marvel at the many different roads we travel in life. And how we oftentimes cross paths with others at the most unexpected moments.

Preparing for departure from the United States on this my last trip here has proved to be both exciting, rewarding and frightful. The war still rages in Europe and I do not relish the idea of sitting in my life-saving India rubber suit while a German submarine might chase us about.

Since the English and American ship lines are considered out of the question for women, I have chosen a Spanish vessel for my return to Europe. I secured a cabin in a ship of about ten thousand tons, not in its early youth by any means. Because of the size of this small ship, I must send most of my trunks on another line — of British registry — and hope that a submarine does not send it to the bottom.

I have had to pack so many seagoing trunks with memorabilia that I have collected during my many visits to America that I find myself somewhat shocked at the large collection of things and writings.

What I have not told anyone is that I plan to retire upon arrival in England, and when the war is ended, to move to

Monte Carlo in the South of France, where the weather is warm and the place is a rendezvous of the world.

I was thrilled last night at the wonderful supper club in this city, Belasco's, to visit with Richard Le Gallienne, who has written a fine poem for my departure from America. I write it down here so that I may always have it.

To Mrs. Langtry on her Departure from America.
I do not bring you flowers,
Or singing birds,
To say farewell,
Nor even words;
Nor to the altar of your eyes
Do I bring signs;
Such antiquated tribute
To the youth
Of the eternal Spring
I do not bring.
And, surely — stars above! —
I bring you not
That miracle called love:
All I can bring —
The one gift worthy you —
Is to bring back again
The wonder and the joy and the delight
Of mortal eyes that saw a little while
The loveliness immortal. I that am poor in all that is not you,
What can I do
Saving bring you back yourself as offering!
Had I but pain
Then would I bring that too —
Alas! there is no pain

For me and you.
So all bring,
As tribute to your feet
Is that most precious thing
The joy you gave,
Indifferently sweet
As some bright star,
That shines alike on all,
And shines for none alone;
Shines but for shinings' sake
In the high heaven afar.
Fair star, too soon to sink
Behind the sea,
My little hoard of star-dust
Here I bring,
As offering:
You unto you — from me.

RICHARD LE GALLIENNE

As though that was not enough to please me, imagine my pleasant surprise when Bat Masterson, the same who was a friend and contemporary of Wyatt Earp and Doc Holliday, came by our table and set an appointment to interview me for his newspaper.

Mr. Masterson, too, has taken to living a slower life, "nearing retirement," he said. Although he was offered a U. S. Marshalship by President Theodore Roosevelt — in Arizona Territory, I believe — he declined. Instead he took a post of U. S. Marshal in New York State. He told me he quit that soon, feeling that some young hoodlum would gun him down sooner or later.

He then went to work for the New York *Morning Telegraph* as a sports writer. He loves it. He writes about boxing mostly, and always has a ringside seat for the top fights.

So, I was not sure what Bat would write about when he visited my suite at the hotel this morning. For a man who lived an exciting and legendary life in the Wild West of America, and now writes about boxing, to interview an actress seemed at first highly unusual. I can easily understand Bat Masterson, the man who was accused of excessive gunplay while acting as marshal or sheriff of Dodge City. Unquestionably, the badmen back then needed a Bat and a Wyatt and the others to control their "excessive" gunplay.

But for this day, let me first record that Mr. Masterson has aged, as we all have. When I first met him some twenty-five years ago, he was a dapper, handsome young dandy who seemed always to wear a dark bowler hat set off, of course, by the pistol on his hip.

Today, he is still handsome, but I fear the raging winds of the West have sanded his features with the dust of the plains, and the beating, exceedingly hot sun that never seems to relax have burned his skin so that it seems chiseled and hardened.

Still, he smiles broadly and his eyes flash with the heat of a man on the path of success.

He entered my suite slowly, his eyes roving about as though he were entering a strange saloon.

"Mr. Masterson, I presume," I called out, for I was in the boudoir at the time of his arrival. Beverly had announced him and then departed for the hotel caterer's to bring back some food and drink for us.

He was gracious to a fault. "Mrs. Langtry," he said.

I stood and smiled to him, feeling every memory I have had of this wonderful land swell over me again. "Bat

204

Masterson. I haven't seen you since those long-ago days in the West."

He chuckled lightly. "Well, that does make it a spell."

I walked him to the front room and we sat alongside each other in the hotel's somewhat uncomfortable chesterfield. He seemed subdued, not the Bat Masterson I had known for those few short days in Tombstone.

"It's a pleasure to see you again, ma'am," he said. "When one of our young lady reporters in the entertainment department — you may know her — name's Louella Parsons — tried to wangle an assignment to interview you, I pulled rank — age has its privileges — and got the opportunity to talk to you for myself. I couldn't let a once in a lifetime chance to see you again go by."

"I'm delighted. So, what shall we talk about?" I asked, trying to put him at ease.

"Lillie Langtry," he answered. "And your plans for the future."

I told him that I was returning to London, that I would wait out the war there and then move to Monte Carlo.

His eyes lit up. "I hear tell that Monte Carlo is an exciting place where one can be ruined faster than it takes to spin a roulette wheel."

I laughed. "Why Bat Masterson," I exhorted, "do you supposed that there's much left of me to ruin?"

He winced at that line and I laughed lightly again. He seemed to become mellow at that point. "Mrs. Langtry," he began, but I interrupted.

"Lillie," I said. "Please."

"Lillie," he continued, "I only meant that the French themselves seem to think Monte Carlo is a gambler's delight upon the Riviera where one could lose one's holdings.

And, as you know, I love to gamble and most certainly appreciate the French appraisal."

"Well, sir," I replied, "one gambler risks his money and another takes it. I am, therefore, safe, since I am not a gambler although I will admit to placing a wager or two on my race horses."

He laughed and said, "Ah, I see why you have been such a huge success in America. But I fear for you because the temptation in a gambling town for those with idle hours, such as you plan on, is not unlike a man seeking to play with fire because there is nothing else to do."

"Thank you for your concern," I said. Then I continued with a bit of philosophy about gambling and Monte Carlo. I hoped at the moment to defend the small French resort for I dearly love the climate and the people there, and will live there no matter. "Naturally," I said, "if one plays with fire one is apt to burn oneself, and it is only unreasoning people who imagine that Monte Carlo, with its luxurious gardens and sumptuous Casino, is maintained to enrich visitors. But there are occasionally very large sums won and taken away by people who are wise enough to leave before they lose their money, for the pendulum swings invariably from good luck to bad in gambling."

"As in life," he added, a comment that I found very true and shall always add to my own analysis of gambling in the future.

Beverly arrived just then and spread out a tray of delicacies that we each enjoyed, including some excellent wine from the ranch and vineyards I formerly owned in California.

When we had taken this respite, he asked me pointedly, "Lillie, will you clear up all the scandalous articles, the rumors, the vitriol that has poured forth about you for the past thirty years? I mean that which we have seen from the lower class of journalists — should they be permitted to call themselves that — concerning you and the Prince."

I was, needless to say, taken aback. The last question I expected from the Marshal of Dodge City, from the rough and tough gambler of Wyatt Earp's Oriental Saloon in Tombstone, was a question about that awful fabrication about the Prince of Wales and me. I don't know how long it took me to form my answer because I excused myself for a moment to wash my hands after Beverly retrieved the empty tray and glasses.

I did indeed go to the powder room and sit and stare into the mirror for a long time. Must I continue with this question the rest of my life? Must I always defend our relationship from the innuendos that have continually followed me? Even the minor ones, such as insisting that I did *not* put the ice down the Prince's back at that dreadful party? More importantly, must I continue to claim that I did not have an affair with Alexandra's husband?

I remember taking some deep breaths, for I felt a tightness in my chest and around my throat while I thought this through. When finally, it having taken longer than I wanted, I formed my answer, I returned to Mr. Masterson, who must have felt I had tested his patience, he being known for not having much.

"I am sorry," I apologized, "for taking so long."

"I hardly noticed," he said, ever the gentleman.

"Mr. Masterson," I began, "a weird story has pursued me through life to the effect that I once, at a supper party in those days, so forgot my manners as to drop a piece of ice down the Prince of Wales' back."

"Yes, that much I have read."

"The tale has become so generally believed that I may be excused for not only alluding to it and emphatically denying it in toto, but for relating at the same time the true story of the incident which gave rise to this silly false one."

He pulled out his pencil, finally, for I began to think he was the kind of reporter who committed everything to memory and then got most of the interview mixed up. "Yes, please, go on."

"One of the most admired women among those I have known during my life was at a ball. It was the small hours, and her waiting husband was getting bored. He hunted for his wife and found her, very wide awake, surrounded by a bevy of admirers, thoroughly enjoying herself. His suggestion that they should go home was, therefore, not received with enthusiasm. As he persisted, and waxed rather warm in argument, she, when his back was turned, deftly popped a spoonful of strawberry-ice down his spine to settle the question. This defiance of marital authority was seen by many, and, being repeated as a good story, found its way into the society papers with no names attached, and later became the foundation for the vulgar fabrication which I have seen in print over and over again, and in which, I repeat, there is not a grain of truth."

"So, the stories about you and the Prince, came from this ball?"

"Yes. But there is more, the unreported part. This was not the only occasion on which this audacious Irish beauty bested her devoted husband, for, going one evening to dine at their house with five or six congenial spirits, I noticed that his place at the table was unoccupied. No apology was offered nor allusion made to the circumstance until later in the meal, when the wine came to an end, and our hostess thereupon gaily informed us that we could not have any more as, having had a difference of opinion with our absent host, she had watched her opportunity and locked the poor man up in the wine cellar!"

Mr. Masterson broke up laughing. "Lillie, that's perfect. Perfect! A sports writer with a tale like this can really get his readers back on the straight and narrow. You have a wonderful sense of timing, a great sense of reality and you are, my dear friend, a true lady."

I stood then, wishing to use the rest of the day to prepare for my departure aboard the Spanish ship on the morrow, and said, "Thank you. You sir, are the finest gentleman in America that I have yet met."

"But how can this be? You met President Grant once. And President Roosevelt. You have met every great leader of my time and many a man otherwise."

"None have been as perfect as you when it comes to treating a lady like the lady she should be."

He was marvelously gracious. He bowed his head slightly and backed out of the room and through the door.

After he had left I plopped back into the chesterfield and stared hard at the wall. I would be happy to return to London, to finally settle in Monte Carlo, to be rid of the need to tell the same Prince of Wales story again and again, because what happened between Edward and me shall always remain a secret — ours alone to cherish.

It is hard to imagine that the suave Bat Masterson, now of New York City, was at one time the most feared gunfighter in all of America. Ah, but that is what makes this country so unique and so unforgettable. I shall miss my adopted country.

24

A Final Entry

Lillie Langtry's folder of papers also included a list of names of people she had met, along with reminders to herself about who they were and that she wanted to send them letters or a "thank-you" note after her final voyage from America to England. The papers upon which these notes were written were partially water damaged, so the list may or may not be complete, since I could not decipher what the damaged papers had written on them.

Some of the notes were addressed to Beverly, upon whom she entrusted much of her secretarial work. Others were "addressed" to herself as though she were a third party.

At first, I was not going to include the list in this book, but I have since decided to publish the entire contents of her packet of papers. I believe that you, like I did, will find these notes interesting, sometimes intriguing.

The following is in Lillie Langtry's own words.

— DLH

My personal thank you for hospitality while in America must be sent to the following:

Mary Harris "Mother" Jones. She is the Colorado labor leader I met who is doing so much for women's rights.

Harriet Quimby, for the thrilling flight in her airplane. I must admit to her I was scared to death. But to fly with the world's first licensed woman pilot was indeed a timeless luxury.

Lynne Fontaine and her new husband, dear Alfred Lunt, with whom I acted so many times.

Lillian Russell

Adelina Patti. Must clarify for her that she is forgiven for bumping me from my scheduled performance at the opera house in Los Angeles so she could give her first concert.

Enrico Caruso, an incredible man with a singing voice that would make all of the world stand and salute.

Somerset Maugham, a brilliant writer.

Maurice Barrymore, an actor from whom I have learned so much.

Adolph Zukor, who permitted me to play act in one of his movies. It was so much fun I wish movies had begun years before.

Douglas Fairbanks, a dashing gentleman who dearly loves pretty women, which, he flatteringly declared, I was the prettiest.

Rudolph Valentino who introduced me to the finest medical doctor yet, a young man in Los Angeles who I must also send regards to. His name was Dr. Robert Griffith.

Pierre Lorillard, the gentleman who invented the tuxedo and also, I suppose because he owned a huge tobacco and cigarette plant, thought my smoking in public was genuine.

President Teddy Roosevelt. He came to my play in Baltimore and the following day walked me through the White House.

Mark Twain, for keeping me so delighted while traveling through the California mining towns.

P. T. Barnum, a boisterous man who also dearly loved my performances.

Henry Ford, for the wonderful ride in his latest auto car. I must have one of my own.

(Ed. Note: The above was the only list with personal notes. The following was a longer list of names of people Lillie apparently knew, some, I assume, from her own country and others from America and France — where she retired. My occasional notes are in parenthesis).

Winston Churchill
Rudyard Kipling
Scott Joplin
J. Pierpont Morgan
Carrie Nation
Andrew Carnegie
Henri de Toulouse-Lautrec
Guglielmo Marconi
Thomas Edison
Emile Zola
Susan B. Anthony
James A. Whistler
Joseph Pulitzer
Pierre and Marie Curie
Frederic-Auguste Bartholdi (sculptor of Statue of Liberty)
Kaiser Wilhelm (Bertie's nephew)
Jules Verne

THE DIARY OF LILLIE LANGTRY

George Bernard Shaw
Maude Adams (actress)
Ruth S. Dennis (dancer)
Stanford White (architect)
Evelyn Nesbit (actress, wife of Harry Thaw who fatally shot Stanford White)
Booker T. Washington
Mary Baker Eddy
Luisa Tetrazzini (opera singer)
Geronimo
Mary Pickford
Emmiline Pankhurst (British suffragette)
Sigmund Freud
Florence Nightingale (died in London at 90 in 1910)
Oscar Hammerstein
Victor Herbert
Vaslav Nijinsky
John D. Rockefeller
Ty Cobb
Isadora Duncan
Charlie Chaplin

Lillie Langtry's letter to Jeannette Rankin, which follows in its entirety, was the only complete letter found among the above-mentioned notes and quite likely was typical of the letters she was planning to write to many of the persons on her rather extensive list.

Dear Congresswoman Rankin,
Please accept my gracious thank you for your hospitality when I visited Butte, Montana. You asked at that time what my thoughts about America were and what I believed, from my perspective as a British citizen, was necessary to

preserve the strength of this great nation. I mean no offense in any of what I write here, since I dearly love America and each American I have met.

I have spent more than thirty-five years visiting America during many exciting and wonderfully fulfilling tours. Many of those years were spent traveling through the Western states, where I was able to meet what I now believe to have been the strongest willed, most individually driven people on earth. Men like Teddy Roosevelt, Lew Wallace, Wyatt Earp, H.A.W. Tabor, John Fremont and so many others. Women like Lotta Crabtree, Helen Modjeska, the delightful Moon sisters and, of course you, the country's first woman in Congress.

To survive the elements the way the American pioneers did, to settle an unsettled land, to develop cities like San Francisco, Denver and Missoula, to build railroads and roadways, and to create so many highly productive farms in such a short time, is testament to the vitality of a free people, unencumbered by a tyrannical government. In retrospect, I believe now that the pilgrims and the revolutionists of this country, those who broke away from Mother England, did so because they possessed an inner desire to lead their own lives, and I believe they were right in doing so. They wished at first to escape the oppressive taxes of the English monarchy and the oppressive nature of the Church of England, but found along the way that complete total freedom of the individual is what makes a country and its people strong.

So they came here and built a country that I believe will become the strongest and most desired nation in the world — if you are able to maintain your freedoms and liberties.

During my tours here I have witnessed many changes, including many inventions that help all of mankind that have come from the inventive Americans. The most recent of course are the automobile and the aeroplane.

But there have been others, including mechanized farm equipment, ginning mills, cotton weavers, steam engines, powered ships and boats — plus too many others to mention.

And Americans seem to love tall buildings like those now rising in New York City. It won't be long before other cities copy New York, each having its own section of "skyscrapers," as they are so aptly called. These symbols of strength are good for you and for your country because they demonstrate to the rest of the world that you are a free country, run by the people.

I have witnessed women's right to have their own personal freedom progress more rapidly in America than in any other country, especially my own, where women are still relegated to the house chores. But I believe you need to free women even more. They deserve the vote, deserve to have jobs alongside men with equal pay for equal efforts.

I have seen the coming of moving pictures and have heard, while playing a part in Adolph Zukor's new movie, that someday these moving pictures will also "talk." Imagine, moving pictures with people talking. Because it is coming from America, I believe it will happen. Unfortunately, such an invention may destroy the theater as I have known it, but it is difficult and unwise to stand in the way of progress.

I guess I feel like a mountain climber. The higher the mountain climber goes, the more he is able to see. Well, Miss Rankin, the older I get, the better is my view of the world. Consequently, because I am old enough now to have lived a full and exciting life, a life that has traveled the world, a life unlike most others I have read about or known, a life that now understands the pattern developing here, I feel a deep attachment to America, to the point of having sought to become a citizen of the great nation that it is.

I want this country to remain alive, vibrant, full of self-directed individuals who invent, build, create and generally bring into the world the thrills of life that are otherwise unavailable anywhere else in the world. That is my dream for your — *our* — America.

I must run now. Beverly has just announced that we must depart for the ship that will take me home. I will write from England again. I do pray that you succeed in your mission as a Congresswoman. I admire you, and believe you hold the future of the country in your hands.

Until we meet again, I remain faithfully yours,

(s) Lillie

The End

From Arrowhead Classics. . .